DREAMERS

DREAMERS
When Worlds Collide

Maynard Tait

ISBN, paperback: 978-1-80227-151-5
ISBN, ebook: 978-1-80227-152-2

This book is typeset in Berylium

Dedicated to my three wonderful children.
The real Joel, Chris and Caitlin.
The inspiration for this fanciful tale.

Live your dreams.

CONTENTS

Chapter 1 11

Chapter 2 19

Chapter 3 29

Chapter 4 41

Chapter 5 59

Chapter 6 69

Chapter 7 79

Chapter 8 93

Chapter 9 101

Chapter 10 111

Chapter 11 121

Chapter 12 137

Chapter 13 145

Chapter 14 155

Chapter 15 167

Chapter 16 181

Chapter 17 189

Chapter 18 203

Chapter 19 221

Chapter 20 233

Chapter 21 249

PART ONE

CHAPTER 1

The chase was on. Joel threw his immaculately hair-styled head around to see if his enemies were gaining on him.

They were – and fast.

His one-man hovercraft was no match for the ultra-speedy sea-doo's that were catching him. The choppy waters made it difficult to accelerate but he was determined to escape with the stolen memory stick held tightly in his left hand. It contained all the secret locations of Professor Pratt's laboratories, and it was the information he had been searching for for months, and now that he had it there was no way he was going to let his arch-rival's henchmen take it from him.

He pulled back even harder on the throttle with his right hand, in a vain attempt to make his craft go faster.

Once again, Joel Swift was running for this life.

'I must get this information back to headquarters if I'm to save the world,' his inner thoughts battling to be heard over the noise of the engine.

Another glance behind him proved that he had to do something immediately or he'd be caught.

Spotting a boat ramp to his right, he shoved the memory stick into his mouth and swallowed hard, threw his left hand down onto the directional control and turned the hovercraft towards the shore.

'They can't follow me up here,' he thought with a smile.

The sun was setting level with the boat ramp and Joel aimed for the orange glow, feeling his safety was assured. His craft thumped onto the ramp and glided along it for a further twenty metres before coming to a sudden halt on a smooth tarmac road. Joel vaulted from his seat like an Olympic gymnast and landed perfectly on the soles of his feet. His wetsuit was suddenly dry to the touch and his now dry, well-coiffured hair waved delicately in the oncoming breeze, all simply from the thought of it happening.

He looked towards the water hoping to find his pursuers sitting on their Sea-Doo's with their fists raised in anger knowing they couldn't follow him – but instead he spotted two unmanned gyrocopters coming his way with machine guns mounted on their sides aimed directly at him. With gritty determination, Joel spun himself around on the soles of his feet, blinked, and smiled as his eyes fell on the red Ducati Vyper motorbike that stood before him, its twelve-hundred-cylinder capacity engine already purring ready for action.

'Nice!' Joel grinned as he leapt onto it; his wetsuit transforming seamlessly into shiny black bike leathers that creaked as they nestled against the seat. Kicking the bike stand up, Joel spun his head around to face the incoming gyrocopters.

'Come and get me – if you can,' he said with a grin.

Joel closed the visor on the safety helmet that now enveloped his head, turned the grip on the handlebars and the bike sped away, kicking up dust and leaving a thirty-foot skid mark behind. The road was completely empty, so Joel twisted the throttle even more and the bike zoomed along at over one hundred miles per hour. In his mirrors he could see the copters still chasing him and they were gaining on him fast.

His eyebrows burrowed low as he wondered what to do. Looking down at his dashboard he spotted a red button with 'EMP Headlamp' written on it.

'Of course!' he thought.

Joel slammed on his brakes and threw the bike into a one-hundred-and-eighty-degree skid, coming to a complete stop in the opposite direction to which he'd just been travelling.

The gyrocopters were nearly on him when a warning message came up on a display on his dashboard. It read 'ENEMY MISSILES LOCKED ON – 10 SECONDS TO RELEASE'.

The countdown continued as Joel threw up his visor before quickly pushing a button on the end of his right-hand handlebar grip.

'9 SECONDS TO RELEASE'

He then pulled back on the grip and the bike's headlamp slowly tilted upwards.

'6 SECONDS TO RELEASE'

He turned the handlebars slightly to the left.

'4 SECONDs...'

He turned the right-hand grip again to lift the headlamp even higher until it was in line with the copters.

'2...'

Joel fixed his gaze on the copters, his eyes wide, and thumped his left hand down on the horn button just as the screen read '1...'.

Joel felt his motorcycle rock ever so slightly as the electro-magnetic pulse pushed its way out of the modified headlamp towards both gyrocopters, knocking out the power to their engines and missiles just in the nick of time. The two lifeless copters fell to the ground and exploded in unison on opposite sides of the road to where Joel sat. Flames rose high into the sky, and he could feel the intense heat forcing its way through his leather jacket.

As Joel contemplated this close encounter a voice entered his ears.

'Agent Swift. Are you there?'

'Yes, I'm here, Agent Smith,' replied Joel with relief. 'Safe and sound.'

'Good. Do you have the information?'

'Yes, I have it.' Joel reached into his jacket and pulled out a packet of gum. He pulled out each slice carefully in case he activated any of the gadgets that had been specially designed for him and secreted into the gum, until he found one labelled 'Minty Mouth'. He removed the wrapper and popped it in his mouth and chewed vigorously.

'Excellent,' said Agent Smith. 'Have you committed it to memory as well as onto a secure memory stick?'

Joel chuckled to himself before replying. 'Er, yeah. I suppose you could say I've digested it - in a manner of speaking.'

'Wonderful, Agent Swift – you'd better come home immediately. Professor Pratt won't rest until he gets that memory stick back. You may be in danger.'

'No kiddin',' he chuckled. 'I'm on my way,' said Joel. 'Pratt hasn't caught me yet and he never will.'

Just as the last word left Joel's mouth, he heard the roar of more engines and, as if out of nowhere, four jet black quad bikes leapt from the fields on either side of him.

'Sorry, Agent Smith,' Joel shouted. 'I'd love to chat, but I've got company – wouldn't want to be rude to my guests'. And with that Joel closed his visor, kicked his motorcycle into life and rode off as fast as he could, closely followed by his pursuers.

The quad bikes bounded across the fields in hot pursuit and Joel thought he'd get away easily, but the road ahead of him ended abruptly and his motorcycle, which was very well designed for the road, now had to contend with the bumps and ditches of the grassy moorland he now found himself riding across.

'This isn't exactly easy,' thought Joel. 'I need something a bit more suitable.' In the blink of an eye and the press of yet another button, Joel's road bike immediately turned into a dirt bike, and it jumped from mound to mound like a leaping gazelle. But the quad bikes were gaining on him, and they seemed to be corralling him into a dead end. He couldn't go left or right, only straight ahead, and then his eyes fell on a lone, spindly figure that stood on a small hill in front of him. It was his nemesis – Professor Pratt.

Joel suddenly became aware that he was trapped and the only way he could go was up the hill without knowing what was on the other side. He pulled back on the throttle, his tyres spitting up grass behind him and the bike aimed directly at Professor Pratt. Pratt, however, dived out of the way and Joel could hear him laugh as his bike left the ground at the top of the hill and dove towards a large net that was waiting for him on the other side. Joel blinked hard and the bike instantly disappeared, but Joel landed in the centre of the net and was then immediately grabbed by several of Pratt's henchmen, all before he could think of an escape route.

Professor Pratt stood at the top of the hill once more and waited patiently as Joel was dragged before him by two gorilla-type thugs and thrown onto the ground in front of him.

Pratt towered over Joel's teenage frame with his hands on his hips, his skinny, bony body jutting out through his pinstriped suit; his thin wiry moustache looking even greasier than the last time Joel had seen him. He wore a black fedora hat which accompanied the long black trench coat.

'Well, well, well,' said Pratt in his plumy English accent. 'If it isn't little Agent Swift I see before me. I never thought I'd have the pleasure.'

'This is no pleasure, Pratt,' said Joel in defence.

'Not for you, Agent Swift, but it is for me.' Pratt bent down and leant into Joel's face, almost doubling himself over as he did so. 'Where is it, Swift?' asked Pratt in an angry, impatient manner.

'Where's what?' replied Joel, trying to delay the inevitable.

Pratt's face contorted until his eyes were barely visible through the slits in his eyelids and his nostrils engorged to twice their size - a large solid bogey becoming visible. Joel just hoped Pratt didn't become any more agitated in case the bogey was dislodged, and it fell into his eye.

'You know what, Swift,' Pratt spat out. 'The memory stick.'

'You'll never get it,' said Joel. 'I swallowed it.'

Professor Pratt stood bolt upright and put his long, bony hands back on his hips.

'You did, eh! Well, my boy, it looks like we'll just have to get it out of you then, doesn't it?'

Pratt turned to two of his henchmen and ordered them to turn Joel upside down and shake him about a bit until Joel coughed the memory stick out. The two extremely fat, but strong men grabbed Joel by the ankles, turned him upside down and shook him violently. Pratt crouched down level with Joel's face.

'Come on, now, Agent Swift. There's no need to be silly about this. Just puke it up and we'll let you go.'

17

'Never! I'm going to get this information to headquarters if it's the last thing I do. And after I do every agent from the Secret Narcoleptic Operations Team will be after you.'

Pratt looked puzzled initially then burst out laughing.

'Ha, ha, ha!' he cackled. 'That's who you work for!'

'Yes,' Joel replied, wondering what was so funny. 'Why?'

'You work for…SNOT,' laughed Pratt.

Joel hadn't realised this before and thought that maybe it was time to work for a different organisation or at least to ask his boss to consider changing the company name.

Pratt pulled himself together and reordered his men to keep shaking Joel.

'Come on! Spit it out,' he shouted.

'No! Never,' Joel responded. 'I'll get away from you, Pratt – I always do.'

'Come on, come on'.

'No, I won't. I won't.'

The shaking continued.

'Come on," Pratt shouted. "Come on. COME ON!'

CHAPTER 2

All Joel could hear was a voice calling 'come on, come on', when his eyes abruptly opened to find his younger brother, Chris, straddled across him shaking him hard.

'Come on, Joel. Wake up, you twonk.'

Joel looked around and realised he was still in his bed. His dreams were becoming more and more intense and harder to wake up from and this last one was no exception. Chris kept on shouting at him and shaking him even though he could clearly see that his big brother was now awake.

'Come on, Joel – its eight thirty. We're going to miss the school bus again. Come on. Get up, barf-face! If I can get back from my dreams in time, then so can you. Come on – bust a move, you big lug.'

Joel grabbed his little brother by the arms and pushed him off the bed before looking at his bed-side clock. It was eight thirty-one. That meant they only had four minutes to get up, dressed and run the two hundred metres to the bus stop.

'Oh no,' Joel mumbled. 'Not again.'

The two brothers dashed around the bedroom looking for their own clothes, bumping into each other on more than one occasion trying to find matching pairs of socks. Their room looked as though a bomb had exploded in it.

They had gotten used to living like this because a tidy room wasn't the most important thing to them. In fact, this world wasn't overly important to them. Sure, they loved living and having a good time whenever they could – which wasn't very often - but their best times were when they were asleep and dreaming.

The Swift children were cursed – or blessed depending on how you look at it - with the most vivid dreams, and they found them more exciting and real than reality itself. At least in their dreams everything worked out how they wanted it to – well, most of the time. Lately, however, their dreams seemed to be taking over.

Joel grabbed a black sock that looked like one of his, but he wasn't quite sure. He threw himself backwards onto his bed, lifted his right leg and pulled on the sock just as Chris shouted at him.

'No! Not that one – I put itching powder in it.'

But his warning was too late. Joel began to grab his foot and roll around on the bed, scratching his toes madly.

'Ow, ow, ow! Ahhhhh! You little twerp. What'd you put it in

here for?' Joel groaned, as he fell off the bed onto the floor with a thud; the guilty sock being flung in the opposite direction.

'Sorry,' Chris offered, pulling on his trousers. 'I was going to swap it with one of Billy Bonce's during gym class today for putting one of my whoopee cushions on Mrs Wilson's seat in Maths yesterday. The poop-face wrote 'PROPERTY OF CHRIS SWIFT' on it. I had to stay in during lunchtime play and clean out Mrs Wilson's guinea pigs – ugh!' Chris stuck his tongue out and wobbled his body as if he'd had a tin of jellied eels poured down his back. 'I hate guinea pigs – and I hate Billy Bonce too.'

Chris had a penchant for practical jokes and took any advantage to play a prank on anyone who crossed him. He may be only nine years old, but he has the devious mind of any teenager. Billy Bonce is his worst enemy and Chris would think of any excuse to prank him.

Joel managed to get up onto his non-itching foot and hop across the room to his chest of drawers and find a clean pair of socks.

'Come on, hurry up,' he said. 'We've only got two minutes to run the length of the street.'

Fully dressed, the two boys rushed to the front door, their book bags swinging wildly as they swung them onto their backs.

'Wait!' yelled Chris as Joel opened the front door. 'We've forgotten something.'

'What?' asked Joel as Chris turned to run back down the hall.

'Our lunch!'

'Forget lunch – we can buy something from the canteen. Come on – we've only got forty-five seconds.'

Chris turned and chased Joel outside slamming the door behind him just as the school bus passed the driveway; its rowdy passengers on the top deck pointing at the two brothers and pulling faces in their direction.

'Quick! Run,' shouted Joel.

The boys ran along the pavement trying to catch up with the bus, dodging young mothers and their pushchairs as they walked to the nursery school at the end of the street. Chris accidentally bumped into one of the prams as he ran. The jolt was enough to knock the baby's rattle out of the pram and into the air. Seeing it above his head Joel put his hands out and caught it. However, he had no time to return it to its rightful owner, as the bus began to indicate and pull over at the stop.

'Sorry!' Chris shouted over his shoulder to the angry mother who was verbally chastising the two as they ran.

The bus had now stopped. They had to run as fast as they could if they were to catch it. Some boys at the back of the bus waved at them to hurry up, but their accompanying smiles were mocking. Joel and Chris were nearly there when suddenly a car reversed out of its driveway across the pavement causing them to make the most of the rubber grips on the soles of their shoes.

They gestured to the elderly driver to move out of the way, but the driver just waved back and smiled as he slowly backed his car onto the road.

Joel looked up and saw the bus indicating right as it was about to pull away.

'No, no, NO!' he shouted.

With the car out of the way the boys burst into a sprint, but it was too late. The bus pulled away too fast for them to jump on. They looked up and saw the boys at the back laughing with a couple of them sucking their thumbs like babies, and then Joel realised he was still holding the baby's rattle in his hand.

He quickly put his hand behind his back. One of the boys on the bus opened a window.

'Forget to set your alarm clock again, Swifts,' he shouted down at them.

Joel and Chris stood panting on the pavement - embarrassed. The boy on the bus shouted again.

'And you've forgotten something else, an' all, aven't you boys.'

'Eh?' said Joel surprisingly, his eyebrows wrinkling.

'What's he on about?' asked Chris.

The boy cupped his hands together to make sure he could be heard as the bus got further away.

'You've only gone and forgotten your sister again,' he laughed.

The whole bus seemed to burst into laughter as it turned a corner and went out of sight.

Joel's mouth dropped open, and his eyes went wide.

'Oh, pants – not again.'

The more times Joel woke up late for school, the more he forgot about his younger sister who was now left at home alone – no doubt in her own dream world and very, very safe, but the thought of leaving her behind again was something Joel was finding hard to deal with. It was happening too often.

'How can I be so stupid?' he said crossly as he turned to walk back home.

'It's not your fault,' said Chris comfortingly. 'I know it's hard to come out of our dreams sometimes. To be honest, I'd only just woken up myself before I jumped on top of you earlier.'

'It *is* my fault, Chris. Uncle Paul and Aunt Sue leave me in charge when they're gone, so Caitlin is *my* responsibility – I should be looking after her.'

Just then the mother with the pram blocked the boys' path. She scowled at them both then reached out and snatched her baby's rattle from Joel's hand before storming off. The baby caught Joel's eye and it blew a raspberry at him then giggled.

Both boys sighed then ran back to the house to get their little sister.

'How are we going to get in past old Baggy Trousers this time, Joel?' asked Chris as they ran, referring to the Headmaster of Binkleford Prep School.

'We've done it before, we'll do it again,' he replied.

'But the last time we were late, he told us we'd be in big trouble.'

'Yes, I know,' said Joel rather downheartedly. 'I know.'

Once inside the house Chris ran upstairs and opened the bedroom door to find his little sister under her duvet, muttering, but still asleep. She began to punch the duvet and as he reached the side of her bed, she kicked the duvet right off herself and it landed on Chris's head, causing him to lose his footing and fall flat on the floor.

Joel walked in and sat down beside her and shook her gently by the shoulders, not wanting to wake from her dream with a shock. Caitlin suddenly stopped thrashing around and opened her big brown eyes.

'Is it morning already?' she asked sleepily.

'Already?' replied Chris sitting up and pulling the duvet off his head. 'Sis, you've been asleep for twelve hours. I think that's plenty of time to dream whatever you were dreaming.'

Joel smiled at her.

'What were you dreaming about anyway? You almost karate kicked your way out of bed.'

'Oh, I was back in Fairy Land and a nasty goblin called Pigface was trying to steal the Fairy Queen's crown, but I was the only one brave enough to try and stop him. We call him Pigface because he's got a big round nose and I know I've seen him before, but I don't know where.'

Chris laughed.

'*You* tried to stop him – that's funny.'

'Why's that funny?' Caitlin frowned.

'Coz you're only little and I've a feeling even the smallest goblin would be bigger than you.'

Caitlin stood up on her bed so that she stood taller than Chris and Joel, grateful for the extra boost to her height.

'I may be little in the real world, but in Fairy Land I'm twice my size and considered a giant amongst all the fairies.'

Chris continued to giggle as he turned and left the room.

'Yeah, okay, whatever you say, Sis. I'll make sure to call on you if I get into trouble in my dreamland of fearless knights and dangerous dragons. Although I haven't had much need for an eight-foot fairy recently.'

'Ignore him,' said Joel gently. 'Did you get the crown back?'

'Of course,' said Caitlin. 'And I sent Pigface packing.'

Joel stood up and opened the curtains, letting the morning sun fill the room.

'Good. Well, come on - you'd better get dressed quickly. I'll make our packed lunches now I'm here,' Joel said, walking to the door. 'We've got to try and get into school without being caught by Mr Porkman, and the later it gets the harder it'll be.'

Caitlin sat on the edge of her bed and looked at her bedside clock, a sad look coming over her face.

'Did you forget me again?' she asked sadly.

Joel turned and looked down at the floor.

'Yes,' he said. 'I am sorry. I won't do it again – I promise.'

'You shouldn't make promises you may not be able to keep,' said Caitlin matter-of-factly.

'But I mean it, Caitlin,' Joel said with a kind smile. 'I promise I won't leave you behind ever again.'

Caitlin hopped off her bed and ran and threw her arms around her big brother's waist. Joel hugged her back, the heavy weight of guilt filling him up as he did so.

The burden of having to look after his younger siblings was taking its toll on Joel, thanks to his over-worked and under-caring guardians. He stood hugging his sister wishing for the umpteenth time that he had his parents back. But it wasn't to be.

Their parents suddenly and mysteriously disappeared a few months after Caitlin was born and the children were put into the care of their father's brother, Paul, and his wife, Sue. Rather reluctantly, Paul and Sue took on the children, although they didn't have a choice seeing as it was what the courts had demanded. Paul and Sue provided everything for the children except the important things - love, attention, and time. All of these they gave to their careers. Paul and Sue weren't exactly child people, and the fact that they had three children thrust upon them, didn't change their views. They were work people and that's why the children loved their dream worlds – it was where everything could be as they wanted it to be, including a happy ending. Usually.

Maynard Tait

CHAPTER 3

Joel, Chris, and Caitlin peered around the gate pillar all at the same time, terrified they would be caught by Mr Porkman as they entered the school driveway.

The last time they were late for school – only two days previously – Mr Porkman gave them one last warning, advising them that if they arrived late once more, they would be expelled – no excuses accepted. Mr Porkman had been gracious even by his standards, having given them twelve warnings already. But, the last time, he meant it. No more chances. He was very aware of the situation with the children's home-life, but he couldn't have them arriving late or falling asleep next to lit Bunsen burners or nodding off during P.E. anymore. There were standards to keep at Binkleford Prep School and the Swifts were lowering those standards. Something Mr Porkman could not stand for any longer.

Joel slowly moved out from behind the pillar and looked all around the empty playground.

'There's no one about,' he whispered. 'If we all go in by the caretaker's room, we can get into the school without passing old Baggy Trousers' office. It's still only nine thirty. If we hurry, we can slip into the back of assembly before it finishes and hopefully no-one will notice.'

'But Stinky Jones will be in there reading his paper,' Chris whispered back. 'He's not usually on his rounds till morning break.'

'We don't need to worry about Stinky,' chuckled Joel. 'I heard him tell Mr Porkman yesterday, while I was returning a bucket and mop to the office, that he had a weakness for white chocolate; so, I've brought a bar with me. He'll be happy to let us through when he gets his hands on it.'

Chris frowned.

'That's odd,' he said to Caitlin. 'Porkman never talks to Stinky.'

'Perhaps Old Baggy Trousers likes chocolate too and they were comparing flavours,' said Caitlin innocently.

Joel waved a hand to Chris and Caitlin, and they followed him slowly across the playground, looking around in various directions, hoping there were no teachers lurking outside having a quick cuppa before classes began.

Just as they approached the caretaker's room and were about to enter it, they heard a car turn into the driveway. They turned around and were shocked to see their uncle and aunt driving in, both with their Bluetooth headsets clamped to the side of their heads and their mouths moving in rapid conversation.

The children ran behind the closest hedge and all three swallowed hard.

'What are they doing here?' asked Chris nervously.

'I don't know,' said Joel. 'But we'd better get a move on. Come on, let's go.'

'I'm scared,' muttered Caitlin.

'Everything will be okay,' Joel replied. 'Come on – we need to go!'

The three of them ran to the caretaker's door; Joel opened it and they piled in one after another to find someone sitting in an armchair reading a newspaper with his back to the door. They all saw the cloth cap on top of his head and sighed with relief – it was Stinky Jones.

Joel put his right index finger to his mouth, indicating to the others to be quiet, as he led them across the cluttered office behind the figure on the chair trying not to disturb him. But just before they reached the door leading to the main corridor, the figure spoke to them.

'Late, are we?' he said in a muffled voice without turning to look at them.

'Er...yes,' said Joel. 'But you don't need to worry about us, Mr Jones. I've got something for you.'

Joel approached the chair from behind and took the bar of chocolate from his pocket.

'I hear you like white chocolate, Mr Jones, so we thought we'd bring you some for all the hard work you do around the school.'

The figure raised its left arm and Joel placed the bar of chocolate into his hand. Chris frowned as he saw the hand's fingers clasp onto it.

'Where did he find that chocolate?' he whispered.

'Enjoy!' said Joel and he turned and walked towards the door ushering Chris and Caitlin ahead of him.

'STOP RIGHT THERE!' the voice growled.

Joel, Chris, and Caitlin stopped and turned around to see Mr Porkman standing up from the armchair wearing Stinky's overcoat and cloth cap; his arm held up high holding the bar of chocolate; his eyes narrow, and a wonky, smug smile on his face.

'I've got you now, Swifts,' he said victoriously. 'TO MY OFFICE,' he bellowed. 'NOW!'

***

Paul and Sue Swift stood by the window in Mr Porkman's office, both having animated conversations into their headsets to complete deals with their clients that should have been taking place in their advertising agency office.

Mr Porkman entered the room in front of Joel, Chris and Caitlin and then motioned to the three children to follow him in and stand next to his desk. He coughed loudly as he walked behind his desk to attract Mr & Mrs Swift's attention, noticing that neither of them paid any notice when he walked in.

They both abruptly finished their phone calls and then turned and faced the children. They stood motionless, staring down at them. They looked cross but as neither of them knew exactly what to say in this situation, they both looked towards Mr Porkman for direction.

Mr Porkman took a deep and audible breath then asked the two adults to sit down in the two armchairs next to his desk.

'I'm sorry to have to say this Mr and Mrs Swift,' Mr Porkman began. 'But as you are aware, last week your children…'

'Er, nephews, Mr Porkman,' Paul corrected nervously.

'And niece,' added Chris boldly.

'Er, yes,' Paul muttered. 'And niece.'

Mr Porkman threw a glare at both adults and children alike and then continued.

'As you are aware, last week your nephews and niece were given one last chance to prove that they are worthy to be pupils here at Binkleford Preparatory. However, since that chance was offered, they have arrived late every morning and fallen asleep in class on several occasions and quite frankly Mr and Mrs Swift this is unacceptable, and they are to be expelled from the school with immediate effect.'

Paul and Sue just sat in their chairs staring at Mr Porkman with eyes as wide as dinner plates unable to think of what to say. They were out of their comfort zone. Give them a meeting with dozens of advertising executives any day and they would find it difficult to stop themselves from talking. But in situations like this, they were as useless as a chocolate teapot. Unfortunately for Joel, Chris and Caitlin, their guardians may have been the best advertising execs in the world, but they were also the lousiest stand-in parents ever. They found any excuse to be at work instead of being at home like normal families. They knew how to sell an advert for the newest model of bicycle or think of a campaign to sell video games to kids, but they simply had no idea how to relate to children – they never had the time nor the inclination.

Mr Porkman leant forward across his desk.

'Mr and Mrs Swift – did you hear what I just said? The children are being expelled. Haven't you anything you want to say?'

Paul's phone chirped into life. He quickly raised it to his ear, answered it, and said he'd ring the caller back then lowered the phone again.

'But we're not teachers, Mr Porkman. We're busy people. I mean we…we haven't got time to look after them during the day. I mean that's what we pay you to do – isn't it?'

'This isn't day-care, Mr Swift – this is a school,' Mr Porkman replied angrily. 'We educate children who are willing to be educated.' He rose to his feet and walked behind the children and put his large, spindly hands on Joel's shoulders. 'We prefer our children to be part of our world when they're here, Mr Swift, but your children…er…nephews and niece prefer to be away off in their own lands of fantasy.' He raised his right arm and waved his hand as if to illustrate the children's mind set.

'Now I know where I've seen Pigface before,' Caitlin blurted out quietly, suddenly staring up at Mr Porkman. 'It's him,' she said nudging Joel's arm. 'He's Pigface! I knew I recognised him in Fairyland.'

Mr Porkman stared crossly down at Caitlin.

'Er, you just remind her of someone, Sir,' Chris said quickly trying to diffuse the moment.

Mr Porkman raised his eyebrows at Paul and Sue.

'This is the fourth school we've tried, Mr Porkman,' Sue said pleadingly. 'You were the only school left that would take them. Couldn't you give them one more chance?' Her phone bleeped loudly, and it was her turn to tell the caller she'd ring back as soon as she was available.

Mr Porkman returned to his chair.

'I'm sorry, Mr and Mrs Swift, but there's nothing more we can do for your children.'

Paul and Sue looked at each other with confusion covering their faces. They then turned to look at the children.

Paul stood up and began to wag his right index finger at Joel in an attempt to look superior.

'You know, Joel, we put a lot of trust in you. We trusted you to look after your brother and sister. It was your responsibility to get them to school on time. That's all we asked of you, just this one thing, and now looked at what's happened. You just can't be trusted anymore, Joel. You always seem to mess it up, don't you?'

Joel's mouth dropped open, the anger boiling up in him. Not once had he ever had the nerve to speak back to his uncle and aunt - usually because they were never around long enough to give him the chance - but now he felt he had to say something. He had to stand up for himself.

'*I* mess it up?' he shouted. 'This isn't my fault. You're meant to be the guardians – not me. And it wasn't just the *one thing*. I'm expected to do everything for us.'

He paused briefly, half expecting a reprimand for talking out, but then realised that neither his uncle nor aunt would know how to reprimand him. They had never been in this position before. The children had always gone along with whatever happened to them. This was something new and it clearly threw them both off guard. So, Joel carried on.

'I buy the groceries; I cook the food; I wash the clothes; I clean the house – heck, I even do all the ironing. And what do I get in return? Nothing. You don't even notice. You both just come in late from work after we've gone to bed and then get up and leave before we've even woken up. Every single day of the week including weekends.'

Joel felt Caitlin slip a hand into his. He looked down at her and she gazed back up at him. He lifted his head and turned to Mr Porkman. 'I'm only a child too, Mr Porkman, who's expected to behave like a grown-up - so don't be surprised if I want to live in my own world once and a while, and there's nothing I can do about it.'

'Nor me,' said Chris defiantly.

'Or me,' Caitlin whispered – smiling up at her big, brave brother.

Paul fell into his seat, shocked at his nephew's ranting, but unsure of how to deal with it. Sue looked embarrassingly from Mr Porkman to the children and then to the floor.

'I honestly don't know what to do,' she said quietly. 'I mean, we can't just quit our jobs – it's what we do best.'

Mr Porkman - who was very aware that the two adults who sat before him were not the best carers in the world, and that the children who he was now expelling were not necessarily the worst he had come across - had an idea.

'Mr and Mrs Swift, may I suggest something?' he asked.

'Please do,' Paul answered with a heavy tone of desperation.

Mr Porkman pulled open the top drawer of his desk and pulled out a small piece of paper and held it in his left hand, frowning at it as he did so, wondering if he was about to do the right thing or not.

'I noticed this advert in the local newspaper a few months ago and it has always intrigued me, which is why I've kept a hold of it. I've never had a reason to refer to it before, but I wonder if this person may be able to help you.'

He passed the piece of paper to Sue, and she held it up for her and Paul to read together.

They read it aloud together.

DORIAN GLASS
SPECIALIST CHILDREN'S TUTOR

CHILDREN ALWAYS SLEEPING?
GOT CHILDREN WITH OVERACTIVE
IMAGINATIONS AND DREAMS?

THEN CALL ME

NOW!

I COULD BE THE ANSWER TO YOUR PROBLEMS
LIVE-IN NECESSARY

TEL BINKLEFORD 7543210

Paul and Sue looked at each other and smiled.

'I suppose we could give it some thought,' said Paul.

'Let's talk about it at home,' Sue replied.

The children looked at each other not understanding what was going on.

'Well, there we are now,' said Mr Porkman rising to his feet and bringing the conversation to an end.

'I do hope you get everything sorted out, Mr and Mrs Swift. I'm sorry it didn't work out here. Goodbye. Goodbye,' he said, practically shoving the whole family out of the office before closing the door behind them.

As soon as the door was closed Mr Porkman literally skipped back to his desk, sat down, and removed the bar of chocolate from his coat pocket that he had taken from Joel. He licked his lips as he ripped off the wrapping, snapped off a large chunk and threw it into his mouth and began to chew the smooth chocolate. Suddenly his eyes nearly popped out of his head and his face went bright purple.

Just as the Swift's reached the front door to the school they heard the most high-pitched wail imaginable followed by someone screaming.

'WATER! WATER! GIVE ME WATER - NOOOOWWWWWWWW!'

Chris stopped in his steps and began to laugh.

'What's so funny?' asked Joel.

'Where did you get that bar of chocolate from?' asked Chris in between chuckles.

'I found it in your top bedside drawer. I didn't have time to get to the shop.'

Chris burst into a fit of hysterics.

'I thought so.'

'Why?' Joel asked.

'Because,' Chris said, still giggling. 'That was my special extra-hot and spicy chilli chocolate. I'd been saving that for a special occasion.'

Caitlin began to chortle too and then Joel joined in as they walked towards the car, leaving Binkleford Prep for the very last time.

Maynard Tait

CHAPTER 4

Paul opened the front door to the house.

'The three of you go straight to your rooms – NOW,' he ordered forcefully – well, as forcefully as he could muster. 'And stay there until the pizza delivery man arrives with dinner.'

He felt slightly awkward, barking at the children. He just wasn't used to it. Any talking that ever took place between he and the children was restricted to the usual niceties like 'Good week at school?' and 'Do you need any extra money to buy anything for the house, Joel?'

Paul and Sue just weren't good communicators with children. They had tried over the years – sort of - but as soon as they took on the role of looking after the children, they just carried on with their jobs at the advertising agency as normal, working alongside each other, initially employing live-in nannies to do all the parenting stuff. They never lost touch with the kids because they were never in touch with them in the first place. Instead, they began to rely heavily on Joel to do almost everything that a normal parent should once the nannies resigned or simply walked out, not knowing how to deal with three sleepy, over-imaginative children.

Joel, Chris, and Caitlin all shuffled off to their bedrooms and left Paul and Sue standing in the hall as they contemplated their next course of action.

'So, what do we do, Paul?' asked Sue. 'Those kids are getting out of control. I just don't know what's gotten into them. Oh, your brother and his wife have a lot to answer for, running off like that.'

'Don't go there, Sue.' Paul interrupted. 'We have no idea what happened to Adam and Tess. They could be dead for all we know.'

'If they were dead, don't you think somebody would've found them by now? Huh? I think they couldn't cope with their own kids, so they ran off leaving us with the lumber. They're probably living it up on some Greek island right now, sipping on tall Iced Teas and topping up their tans.'

'Aw, come on, Sue, knock it off. Adam would never do anything like that. He was always a dependable guy – someone you could trust your life with. He would do anything for his family. And Tess was the perfect mother - always there for her kids – she gave up a lucrative job to be with them twenty-four seven.'

'Yeah? Well, she isn't around anymore and hasn't been for six years, Paul. They left us to pick up the pieces – well, the courts did – but I never asked for this, and I don't intend on becoming Mum of the Year now. These kids need someone who can sort them out. And the sleeping – it's getting worse. All they want to do is sleep. Why is that?' she continued, raising her hands to the ceiling in the vain hope that a higher power than Paul was going to answer her question.

'I don't know,' Paul answered honestly. 'Perhaps Joel was right. Maybe we have been neglectful, maybe it's their way of dealing with the fact that we're not around much.' He began to pace around the hall. 'We've created such a boring life for them that they'd rather create better ones in their dreams, and that's where they find solace and peace.'

Sue stared at her husband.

'That's deep, Paul – even for you,' she said mockingly. 'So, what do you suggest?' she added harshly. 'That one of us quits and stays home and becomes one of those stay-at-home parent types? Uh-uh, no way, Paul - I can't. I'm locked in with the TV campaign for the *Baby Barf* doll for the next few weeks and then I've got to try and seal the deal with *Lucy's Luscious Lipstick*.'

'Well, I can't do it,' Paul replied. 'I've got that meeting in Canada next week with *Sea Shore's Spicy Squid Sticks* and then the meeting in New York with Phil Fluffmann about the *Phil the Fluffer's Favourite Flute and Fiddle* video feature for Tiny Tim's Teatime Tunes on the TTFN channel, followed by the conference in Alabama run by the Alabama and Atlanta Advertising Association Agency.'

Sue stared wide-eyed and drop-jawed at her husband.

'You got the A and A A.A.A. job.' She emphasised every letter. 'Man, I so wanted to go to that this year.'

'It's okay,' smiled Paul reassuringly. 'I'll bring you back some leaflets and information packs – it'll be as though you were there yourself.'

'Aw, thanks sweetheart – you are *so* considerate,' Sue said as she kissed him gently on the lips.

'You're welcome,' said Paul.

After a second smooch followed by a moment's silence, when they're current situation finally came back to their minds, Sue asked, 'So, like I said – what are we going to do?'

Paul reached into his jacket pocket and took out the piece of paper that Mr Porkman had given them.

'It looks like we've no other option. Let's give this Dorian Glass a call.'

***

After their first family mealtime together for weeks, or perhaps months - albeit in front of the shopping channel on the TV while Paul and Sue constantly criticised the way the presenters were trying to sell their goods – Joel, Chris and Caitlin were sent back to their rooms and told to have an early night so that they could be wide awake and ready to meet someone who was coming to see them the following morning.

Caitlin was the first to bed and have her light turned out after being read to and tucked in by Joel. Her room was almost pitch black except for a soft blue glow that was emitted by a plug-in light near the door. She lay under her duvet and blinked her eyes as they adjusted to the darkness. Without moving her head off her pillow, she began to make out shapes caused by the shadows. On top of her wardrobe, she could make out the shape of a dolphin, but she knew it was a folded blanket with a cone-shaped party hat sitting on it. By the window she saw a fat man wearing a bowler hat, but she knew it was just the shadow of her toy tortoise resting on a football.

Caitlin then focused her eyes on a spot on the ceiling. The exact spot she fixed her eyes on every time she wanted to fall asleep. To Caitlin the spot was the shape of a butterfly which helped her to drift off every time she wanted to, and within a few seconds Caitlin's eyes began to close and she entered Fairy Land once more.

As she blinked to let her eyes get accustomed to the beautiful yellow sunshine that poured down upon Fairy City, she noticed the fluttering wings of a butterfly pass over her head. Lifting herself up to rest on her elbows in her leaf bed high in the trees, Caitlin the Fairy smiled a very wide smile as she gazed out at the beautiful kingdom of Fairyland and all the wonderfully bright colours. She could hear the humming wings of other fairies that were already up and busily carrying out their morning chores as she breathed in the intoxicating scent of the gigantic flowers upon which the fairies lived.

She looked to her left and saw Snuzzle her magical unicorn winging his way toward her. Caitlin jumped up onto her feet and flapped her wings only enough to lift her off her leaf and for Snuzzle to fly under her and take her up and away into the sky to start her day.

As Caitlin was transported high across Fairyland, she took in all the beauty of the kingdom and she was proud to be the fairy who everyone counted on to protect them from the evil goblins who tried and tried daily to steal the Queen Fairy's crown, which in turn would give them the power the goblins needed to rule the kingdom. However, since Caitlin had been offered the job of Freedom Enforcer not one goblin had been able to get anywhere near the Queen's palace, let alone inside it. For now, Fairyland was a peaceful place.

Snuzzle turned his neck to his right and began to glide down gracefully, aiming to land on the top of a small hill that overlooked the wide river that separated Fairyland from Goblin Domain. As Snuzzle touched down Caitlin jumped off his back and landed on both feet next to him. She looked all around her in every direction before cupping her hands around her mouth. After taking a deep breath Caitlin began to blow hard and the sound of a hundred long horns seemed to thunder from her mouth. She stopped after only a few seconds and then she looked all around her again. From the east of where she stood, she could see the person she had been calling for rising from behind a hill. Marshmallow Man stood at least twenty metres tall, and he slowly bounded his way towards her, a wide toothless grin appearing on his massive bright pink, podgy face.

Marshmallow Man was pink from head to foot and was Caitlin's goblin bashing assistant, although because of Caitlin's own height she didn't have to call on him very much but having him around helped to make her feel safe.

Caitlin the fairy was also tall. In fact, she was the tallest fairy ever and the main reason she was given the job of Freedom

Enforcer, apart from the fact that she was fearless in the face of danger.

She waved and then fluttered her wings and flew towards him and landed on his soft and springy shoulder. 'Hey Pinky,' she whispered gently. 'It's good to see you again. I don't know why, but I've a funny tingle in my tummy telling me that I'm going to need you later.' She pointed towards the Sapphire City. 'Come on – let's go and see if the Queen has any special orders for me today. Don't want those nasty goblins trying to steal her crown again.'

Marshmallow Man gave Caitlin a gooey smile and bound his way across the luscious green fields while Caitlin made herself comfortable on his shoulder, smiling to herself, happy that nothing could bother her now.

***

Chris jumped onto his bed and pulled his duvet up under his chin, his eyebrows almost meeting in the middle as he frowned heavily.

'Who do you think is coming over tomorrow?' he asked Joel, who was sitting on the window seat staring out into the darkness at nothing in particular.

'Another nanny, I guess,' he replied. 'No school's going to take us now, so we'll probably end up with some smelly old prison warden type and we'll never be able to leave the house.'

Joel was particularly grumpy, as he viewed the current situation as his fault, even though he really knew that his aunt and uncle should take the blame. He felt obliged to look out for his younger siblings knowing that his aunt and uncle weren't up to the job. He bore this responsibility heavily and was annoyed with himself that once again he let his dreams ruin reality.

'It's not your fault, y'know,' said Chris reassuringly. 'We all get wrapped up in our dreams – it's what we do.'

'Yeah, well, perhaps we need to live in the real world a little bit more.'

'Maybe,' said Chris raising a half-smile. 'But where's the fun in that?' He threw his head back onto his pillow and flicked off his bedside lamp. 'Well, I'm bushed. G'night.'

'Night,' said Joel. 'Sweet dreams.'

'I hope so, bro – I hope so.'

Within a minute Chris was fast asleep and he immediately found himself sitting on his trusty steed, Bucktooth, wearing full body armour and holding a lance in his right hand. He peered through the narrow eye slit in his helmet and he realised he was at one end of a jousting field, and at the other end he could see a knight in black armour pointing at him with a very fierce look on his face. Suddenly the knight closed his face guard and kicked both heels into the side of his horse and it lurched forward, beginning its charge down the field – the knight's long menacing lance aimed right at Chris.

Chris could hear the cheers and screams from the huge crowd that surrounded the field and before he could do anything, he heard a voice shout, 'Good luck, Sir Chris' and some other words that he couldn't quite make out. Suddenly his horse reared up onto its hind legs before lunging forward and began its own gallop towards the oncoming knight; the only thing separating them now was a narrow wooden wall.

Chris gripped the reins tightly in his left hand and lowered the lance to a horizontal position with his right. He steadied his right arm and pointed the end of his lance at the black knight. The horses thundered down the field, the sound of their hooves filling Chris's ears, overpowering the noise from the crowd. He leant slightly forward in his saddle and dug his knees into Bucktooth's sides, preparing himself for the inevitable hard jolt he was about to receive. He fixed his eyes on his opponent and gritted his teeth before noticing that the black night had something in his left hand that Chris didn't. A shield.

Chris looked back and spotted his servant, Twurp, jumping up and down furiously, holding his shield.

'Oops!' he thought.

There was only one thing to do. As the two horses drew almost level, Chris removed his left foot from its stirrup and he threw his body to Bucktooth's right side, the tip of the black knight's lance just missing his left shoulder. With all his might, Chris threw his right arm across the front of Bucktooth's head just enough to strike the black knight's shield with his lance.

The black knight wobbled in his saddle but managed to regain his composure and ride to the end of the field, lance and shield intact, and then turn his horse around for the second run. Chris pulled himself up onto his saddle as Bucktooth turned around to prepare to gallop again. Standing behind the black knight at the far end of the field Chris could see Twurp, holding up his shield. Over the noise of the horses' hooves thumping into the ground he could just about hear Twurp shout 'I tried to tell you!'

But Chris had no time to respond as both horses started running at the same time. Chris knew that if he carried out the same manoeuvre again, the King would declare the black knight the winner and he wouldn't win the prize of an afternoon in the company of Princess Patience, something Chris had always wanted. All he had to do was to get the black knight off his saddle and onto the ground, but if Chris jousted in the normal way, he was sure to get a lance full in the chest and be knocked off his horse instead.

Instinctively, Chris threw his lance from his right hand to his left, swapping reins as he did so. The two horses were almost level. Chris saw the steal-tip of the black knight's lance coming right at him. He turned his left shoulder forward, throwing his full weight behind his lance, narrowly escaping a punch to the chest. His lance caught the buckle of the black knight's saddle strapped to the underbelly of his horse. The buckle gave way and Chris let go of his lance for fear of catching the hind legs of the horse as it galloped past him.

Bucktooth slowed to a canter as Chris twisted his head around in time to see the black knight falling off the back of his horse, complete with lance in one hand and shield in the other, his backside landing perfectly on top of his saddle with a thud onto the muddy ground.

The crowd was in hysterics as the black knight's horse came to a stop, turned around and wandered back to its rider before sitting down next to him.

Chris threw his face guard up and looked toward the royal box. The King was clapping heartily and then beckoned Chris and the black knight to come before him. The black knight hobbled toward the King, his right hand rubbing his bruised behind, while Chris trotted Bucktooth over next to him.

'Please dismount, Sir Chris,' the King requested with a smile.

Chris did so and stood elbow to elbow with the black knight - or to be precise, elbow to hip - seeing as Chris was about half the size of the black knight. The sight of the two knights next to one another caused some further laughter amongst the crowd; especially from behind as the black knight continued to rub his extremely sore rear end.

The King raised both hands to ask for silence.

'Sir Chris, I declare you the winner of this morning's games, and for your prize you may accompany my daughter, Princess Patience, on a picnic in the palace gardens this afternoon.'

Chris had been dreaming about this day for a long time and at last he had the chance to spend time with his childhood sweetheart all on his own because usually they were surrounded by all their other school classmates, so it was nice to know that the whole afternoon it would be just the two of them.

The crowd applauded as Chris stared into the beautiful blue eyes of Princess Patience who replied with a shy smile. The King then declared the games over and everyone began to leave.

The black knight followed Chris off the field and as they reached the armour tent, he laid a heavy gauntlet on Chris's shoulder causing him to spin around on his heels. The knight removed his helmet allowing his long black hair to tumble down over his shoulders revealing a rather bushy and alarmingly odd-shaped moustache.

'Too many times you have made a fool of me, young Sir, and in front of their Majesties. I charge you with this, sir, it will not happen again. I am the Prince of Poop Poop, and I shall be the one who will woo Princess Patience – not you.'

Chris took off his helmet and tossed it to Twurp.

'Poop Poop?' repeated Chris, a wry smile emerging. 'That's the name of your land?'

'It's your dream, young Sir,' said the Knight snootily. 'It's what you called my land when you started this charade.'

Chris giggled. 'Oh, yeah – so I did. Nice one.'

'Watch your back, Sir Chris,' threatened the knight as he turned and walked away. 'You haven't seen the last of me.'

'Oh, I hope not,' shouted Chris as the knight walked out of sight. 'You and your girlie hair and bonkers moustache.'

In the blink of an eye Sir Chris was dressed back into his normal everyday clothes – including his snot green tights, his leather boots and his oversized ruff which made his head look like a pea sitting on a white plate. However, this was the height of fashion in this Medieval World and Sir Chris set the standards, in more ways than one. Sir Chris of Scamalot was known to everyone as a charmer, a brave knight, but also a keen prankster. Given any chance Sir Chris would play a trick on anyone just for a laugh, but generally to make nasty and stupid people look even more stupid.

While walking back through the castle market with Twurp he spotted a grotty looking teenager steal the purse from the handbag of one of Princess Patience's ladies-in-waiting as he pretended to accidentally bump into her. The boy apologised to the lady before turning on his heels and running right towards Chris.

Chris, who was standing next to a fruit stall, grabbed a huge watermelon and sliced it in half with his hip dagger. In one half he quickly cut two round holes and a crescent moon shape under them. As the boy approached, Chris walloped one half of the melon smack into his face causing him to collapse in a heap on the ground. As he sat up Chris slapped the other half of the melon onto the back of the boy's head, the two halves meeting over his ears.

Everyone in the market laughed as the boy sat dumbfounded with his surprised eyes peering out of the two round holes and his tongue hanging out of the moon shaped hole, like a donkey gasping for water.

'I think that counts as two of your five-a-day,' joked Chris loudly. 'Now hand over the purse, get up and get lost before I consider how to give you the other three.'

The boy tossed the purse into Chris's hands as he jumped to his feet and ran off through the market bumping into nearly all the stalls as he went, everyone laughing hysterically.

Chris walked up to the lady-in-waiting and handed her the purse. She curtsied before him and thanked him repeatedly. But Chris didn't seem to notice her as his eyes rested on Princess

Patience who was standing behind the lady, a broad smile beaming radiantly from her perfect face.

'My lady,' Chris said as he bowed his head gently, the way a gentleman should in the presence of royalty.

Princess Patience curtsied politely and then turned to walk back towards the castle gates, her ladies-in-waiting trotting and giggling behind her, throwing glances behind them in Sir Chris's direction.

Chris stood fixed to the spot – his eyes locked onto the back of the princess's head, a dribble of drool slowly falling from a corner of his mouth. It took three nudges to the ribs from Twurp to bring him out of his trance.

'M'Lord! M'Lord!' Twurp said in his country bumpkin accent. 'Snap owt of it. You'll see 'er later anyways.' He pursed his lips together as if to admit defeat. 'She'll be yer downfall, she will. It's always a girl that brings the good'uns down. You mark my words.'

Chris blinked a few times.

'Oh, Twurp. If only you knew my heart and how it longs to be joined with hers.'

Twurp whacked Chris on the back of his head before grabbing him by an arm to pull him in the opposite direction from the castle.

'Give over, you romantic twonk,' he said matter-of-factly. 'Come on – let's go and get some lunch before yer date with 'er nibs, the Princess. Your heart may be full, but my stomach's empty and needs a pasty.'

Chris almost tripped over himself as he was being dragged away, but he kept looking after Princess Patience with a soppy big grin covering his face.

***

Joel wasn't normally this fed up. The events of the day had really got to him. Although he enjoyed his dreams, he wished that if they were going to be such a part of his life that they could be of use to someone. But they were *his* dreams. 'How could anyone else benefit from my dreams?' he thought to himself.

He sat on the end of his bed wondering what it would be like if his dreams became reality. Things would be easier. He knew what to do in his dreams. If they became real, then he'd be able to cope with anything and he wouldn't have to worry about things like self-doubt or feeling useless.

With a deep sigh he got into bed. He noticed that Chris must have been having a good dream because he had a dopey smile on his face, and he was drooling from the corner of his mouth.

'Princess Patience again, I suspect,' he whispered.

He clicked his bedside lamp off and lay his head down onto his pillow. As soon as he closed his eyes, he began to think of how his dream would start. He didn't want it to begin with him in the clutches of the evil Professor Pratt or his henchmen – that usually came towards the end of his dreams. But as he'd been woken so abruptly earlier that morning by Chris, he thought it may start in the same place, so he began to imagine himself nearing the top of a rock face on a cool summers evening – somewhere Pratt couldn't reach him.

No sooner had he had this mental picture in his head when he found himself gripped to the side of a sheer rock face. Looking directly in front of him he noticed that a peg had been inserted into the rock which meant he was safely attached and there was no fear of him falling. And when he looked down below, he was very glad about that. It must have been at least two hundred feet down to the tree line below.

'Wow!' he croaked. 'Never been rock-climbing before. I hope the Agency have trained me on this.'

Looking upwards his eyes scanned the cliff-face for the next place to move to. Without much thought he pushed his legs up and stretched his left hand up to a tiny crack in the rock. His fingertips locked onto it, and he pulled himself up stealthily and threw his right hand onto a small ledge.

'Looks like I do know how to climb,' Joel told himself. 'This is fun.'

Joel continued to climb upwards, every move made easily. At one point he stopped to put another peg into the rock to hold himself in position. After he had made himself secure, he turned his head around to take in the magnificent view. The sun was about to set, and the sky was a dusky orange colour. The forest directly below him seemed alive as the tops of the fir trees swayed to and fro in the gentle breeze. A river ran through the forest and the fading light of the day reflected up at him from it. In the far distance he could make out the roof of a building and on the top of it he could just make out the letters S N O T. It was the Agency's headquarters.

'Well, there's no doubt that I'm in the right dream,' he said, smiling.

He then threw his body around to face the giant wall in front of him, looked up and without any hesitation he began to climb nimbly up the mountain wondering what was ahead of him for the rest of the night.

Maynard Tait

CHAPTER 5

Dorian Glass stood on the front step and knocked heavily on the Swift's front door, a solitary plastic bag containing all his possessions, gripped tightly in his left hand. Aware of how people usually react to his unexpected looks on their initial meeting, he had pulled his long, brown hair into a ponytail to try and make himself more presentable, and he had put on a leather necktie even though he wasn't wearing a shirt, just a plain white t-shirt – which was more of a grey colour from not being washed very often - under a very well-worn denim jacket. His faded blue jeans and black cowboy leather boots completed the outfit and gave him the look of an ageing rocker.

Catching his reflection in a glass panel in the door he wished he had had a chance to shave too, but one of the more aggressive guests at the hostel where he had just spent the night decided they wanted his razor, so not wanting to cause a fight he gave it to him. He thought of the many times in the past he had knocked on the doors of prospective families who had called on his services, hoping he would be the solution to their problem children. But after a short while he had found that *they* weren't the right ones for *him*. He wondered and hoped that perhaps this would be the place for him and the children he was about to meet would be the right ones.

The door opened and Paul and Sue stood on their welcome mat and stared out at this man who did not fit their mental picture of a tutor, never mind someone they could trust to leave the children with. Perhaps this wasn't who they were expecting.

'Er…I'm sorry for staring,' said Paul. 'We thought you were someone else. How can we help you?'

'I'm Dorian Glass. You called me last night and asked me to come over at nine.' He lifted his right arm as if to look at a watch, but he didn't have one. 'Well, it's nine and here I am.' He added a warm smile trying to soften the obvious blow to Paul and Sue's expectations.

Even though they both knew it was rude to stare, they just carried on staring at this conspicuous person in front of them, their eyes shifting from his long, greasy hair down to his ripped clothes finally resting on to the strange tattoos on both hands.

In a flash, Paul looked up at Dorian, said, 'Not today thank you' and slammed the door shut.

'Why did you do that?' asked Sue, slightly whispering and slightly angry, not wanting the man on the other side of the door to hear her.

'Why?' Paul asked just as quietly. 'Didn't you see him? He's a tramp! We can't have a tramp come into our home – what would the neighbours say?'

'Okay, so he may look like a tramp, but right now he's our last hope. I appreciate he may not look like your average tutor, but we've got no other choice.'

'But he's got tattoos and…and…he smells,' Paul protested.

'Then he can have a shower and wash his clothes.'

'But how do we even know he's any good? We know nothing about him.'

Suddenly the letter box flap in the door opened and an envelope marked 'References' was pushed through.

'In case you're having doubts,' Dorian shouted from outside.

Sue took the envelope, opened it, and read through the pages of references from previous employers, going back over twelve years. Each one of them gave a glowing report.

An excellent teacher – the children were sorted out in no time, one read.

Outstanding, read another.

A truly gifted man who knows the minds of children. Sorry he had to leave so soon, read the last.

Paul scanned his eyes over them and had to agree that Dorian Glass certainly came highly recommended.

'Okay, okay,' he said. 'We'll give him a week's trial. If the children don't respond to him then he goes. Agreed?'

'Fine,' said Sue.

Paul opened the door. Dorian hadn't moved an inch.

'I... er...apologise about that,' Paul offered. 'It's just that you weren't what we were expecting. No bow-tie or corduroy trousers,' he laughed.

Dorian smiled back.

'It's okay, I never am.'

'Please come in,' said Sue.

Dorian walked in and looked around the cavernous hall, raising his eyebrows.

'I'm Sue Swift and this is my husband, Paul.'

'Nice to meet you,' said Dorian as his eyes fell on a rather large photograph of Paul and Sue holding their 'Advertisers of the Year 2019' award. 'What a lovely home.'

'Oh, thank you,' Sue beamed. 'It's all from hard-earned salaries. Nothing's free these days. If you want it, you gotta work for it, that's what we say – don't we, darling.'

'Absolutely,' Paul replied. 'So, Dorian, don't take this the wrong way and forgive me for being so forward, but what makes you so good at what you do? I mean, we've tried loads of tutors before and none of them have been able to sort our kids out, so what makes you so 'special'?'

Dorian put his bag down by his leg and placed both hands into his jean's pockets. 'Well, I find I can relate to children who would rather spend time in their own imaginations than in the *real world*. I try to see things from their perspective and then I take it from there.'

'Okay,' said Sue rather dubiously. 'So, explain how you do that...exactly.'

'I get to know them and find out why they'd rather be somewhere else than where they are right now, and then I try to bring them back to reality before it's too late.'

Paul and Sue glanced at each other when they heard this.

'Too late?' Paul repeated. 'What do you mean *too late*?'

'Before they believe that their dreams are better than reality, of course,' said Dorian. 'This is their world – this is where they should be. This is where they should live.'

'I see,' said Paul nodding his head up and down – although he had no idea what Dorian was on about. 'Okay, well, here's the deal. We'll give you a week's trial and then we'll see where to go after that. What do you say?'

'Sure thing, Paul,' Dorian replied.

'Well, I suppose you ought to meet the children,' Sue said as she walked to the stairs. 'I'll just go and get them. Knowing them they're probably still all in the land of nod. Paul, can you offer Dorian a drink or something while he waits?'

Paul showed Dorian into the kitchen while Sue walked briskly up the stairs and into the boys' bedroom. Both Joel and Chris were, indeed, still fast asleep, and clearly very happy about it too. Chris had both arms wrapped tightly around his favourite cuddly dog and was kissing it softly on the lips, while Joel lay with his hands behind his head smiling up at the ceiling, his eyes tightly closed.

'Wake up!' she shrieked in a shrill voice, clapping her hands repeatedly.

Both boys woke up groggily. Chris rubbed his eyes and Joel rubbed his head.

'What time is it?' Joel asked.

'It's time you were awake and downstairs. Your new tutor's here and we want to introduce you to him before we leave for work. We're already late as it is.' Sue grabbed the boys' duvets and pulled them off the beds. 'Kitchen – five minutes!'

With that last order Sue left the room and went into Caitlin's room and found her standing on her bed doing martial art moves against thin air - her eyes tight shut. As Sue approached the bed to wake her up Caitlin somersaulted off it and landed on her bean bag, her face plunging into the tummy of a giant teddy bear. Not surprisingly this move was enough to waken her up.

'What happened? Where am I?' she moaned.

'You're at home, in your room and it's time to get up and get dressed. No more karate young lady. I want you in the kitchen in five minutes.'

Sue left Caitlin lying on the beanbag, her eyes rolling around in their sockets.

'Boy, was that goblin tough!' said Caitlin.

***

Joel, Chris, and Caitlin entered the kitchen in various states of dress and yawned widely as they shuffled their way to the breakfast bar. Instinctively, Joel bent down underneath the bar to get a fresh carton of orange juice from the fridge, but he noticed that everything had already been set out.

'Children,' said Sue. 'Before you eat, we'd like you to meet your new tutor. This is Mr Glass and he's going to start today, and he'll move into the spare room. Er…on a week's trial,' she added hastily, looking to Dorian for agreement.

'Please, call me Dorian. And it may not take that long – it all depends on the children,' Dorian said, gazing at each child in turn. His eyes widened and Joel noticed that his pupils seemed rather large which gave him a rather strange and sleepy, but friendly look.

The children all stared back at this weirdly dressed, but gentle looking man. Caitlin, however, although feeling quite calm, still had to reach across and put a hand into Joel's for comfort. They then introduced themselves to him.

Dorian continued to smile at them and then turned to face Paul and Sue.

'I think we're going to be just fine here. Why don't you two head off to work? I'm sure you've both got very busy days ahead of you.' He looked back to the children. 'And so, have we. We'll start by getting to know each other.'

Paul and Sue left rather quickly after saying that Joel knew where everything was and that he'd show Dorian around the place, and that if they needed anything to call their grandmother.

Caitlin smiled at Dorian thinking that this tutor didn't seem like the normal kind of tutor they usually had. Chris frowned at him, his lips pursed trying to get the measure of him, but mainly trying to work out what prank would be a good one to play on him, just so he knew who and what he was dealing with.

Joel just kept on staring. He couldn't quite believe that his uncle and aunt had gone off and left them with this man who they'd only just met ten minutes earlier. Even for them this was unusual. They'd normally quiz prospective tutors for at least an hour and then ask them to come back the next day and tell them whether they'd got the job. Why was this one different?

'You seem concerned, Joel,' Dorian said. 'Don't you trust me?'

Joel's stare remained as he answered.

'How can I trust you – we've only just met.'

'A fair point – and cautious,' Dorian replied. 'But just as your uncle and auntie have done, sometimes you must put your faith in someone and trust they'll do the right thing, instead of thinking you can do it all yourself. That's lesson number one.'

He moved along the counter past Caitlin and looked deeply into Chris's eyes who returned Dorian's inquisitive gaze.

'So, what's your speciality, Chris?' He put a finger to his lips and tapped it a couple of times before answering his own question. 'Hmm! You look like the kind of guy who likes to play games. Am I right?'

Chris's frown disappeared and he shot a glance to Joel and then back to Dorian.

'Er...um...yeah, I like to play. Doesn't every kid?'

'I guess so,' Dorian said lifting a finger to the air and tilting his head to the right. 'Just remember, never play with fire - you might get burned.'

Chris's frown returned, heavier than normal trying to figure out what Dorian meant.

Dorian then moved back to Caitlin, bent down, and rested his head on his hands in front of her. He studied her face carefully noticing out of the corner of his eye her hand in her brother's.

'And Caitlin, are you afraid of me?' he asked gently.

'A little,' she said.

'You don't want to be afraid though, do you?'

'No.'

'So, you're afraid on the outside, but not on the inside – am I right?'

Caitlin nodded in agreement.

'Well, we'll just have to bring the inside Caitlin, outside,' Dorian said kindly.

Caitlin was puzzled by what Dorian has just said and her face showed it.

'Don't worry,' he said with a wink and a smile. 'We'll work on it.'

Dorian stood up and clasped his hands together to gather their attention and their thoughts. 'Okay, so now we've met each other, how about we have some breakfast before we get to the learning.'

Maynard Tait

CHAPTER 6

After breakfast, Joel showed Dorian the spare bedroom. Dorian tipped the contents of his plastic bag onto the bed and put them all into an empty bedside cabinet. He only had three changes of clothes, a notebook, pen, and a wash bag.

'You don't have very much stuff. What are you – homeless?' asked Joel rudely.

Dorian took off his jacket and placed it on the back of a chair beside the window. He was used to the children he taught being rude to him: a stranger coming into their house telling them how and when to do things. It was part of the course. He understood. But he didn't like it.

'Well, I don't *own* a home if that's what you mean, Joel. I'm not technically homeless when I have a job and I don't have the need for *much stuff*, as you put it. I go from one job to the next. If I had more stuff then I'd need to carry another bag, and I like to have one arm loose when I'm walking. It makes me feel free. I don't see the point of carrying too much baggage around with me – no point in burdening myself with unnecessary baggage, now is there?'

'I suppose not,' Joel replied, although the question was rhetorical. He shuffled his feet uncomfortably. 'So, are you just a bad teacher? Is that why you have to move around a lot? Why don't you stay in one place? Haven't you got a family?'

Dorian chuckled at how direct Joel was.

'Actually, I think I'm a pretty good teacher – I've never had a complaint yet. I guess I just haven't found the right place for me, y'know - somewhere to be of real use to people.' He paused then opened his arms wide. 'Who knows – maybe this is it. As for family – no, Joel, I don't have any family here. It's just me.'

'Well, don't get too comfortable,' Joel muttered as he turned to leave the room. 'You'll leave soon enough. They always do.'

'We'll see, Joel. We'll see.'

***

The rest of the day was spent on multiplication, English, and some History. Within an hour Joel had it confirmed that Dorian was a good teacher, as he had claimed. In fact, the children all found him very friendly, easy to listen to and fun. They couldn't remember the last time they'd all laughed together and this new teacher of theirs knew how to make even the most boring subjects' fun. During the history lesson, Dorian made all the children play a character from the time period he was explaining.

'I always think people learn better if they become part of the lesson,' he told them.

And learn they did. Even Caitlin, who hadn't done any history before, found it immense fun to learn about Henry VIII by pretending to be all his six wives, one after the other. Joel also managed to laugh at himself when he tried to portray the fat King by putting on a deep, posh voice.

Chris loved maths especially, because Dorian used a humongous bag of jellybeans as counting units, and every time they got a sum correct, they could eat two of them. Chris had forgotten how much he loved jellybeans.

It was almost six thirty in the evening before they sat down to dinner. While the children did some homework - which Chris cheekily told his new teacher was 'ironic' seeing as all the work they were doing was done at home – Dorian prepared a large bowl of chicken and pasta in cheese sauce. As he sat down at the table to join them, he put a plate of spicy potato wedges and garlic mayonnaise down and within two minutes the plate was cleared, and all the kids chomped on their chicken.

'Thish ish delishish,' Chris mumbled as a blob of mayonnaise slid down his chin.

'Yum, yum,' Caitlin agreed.

Dorian smiled as he threw a wedge into his mouth. 'Glad you like it.'

'Yeah,' said Joel. 'It makes a change to my sloppy mash and burnt sausages.'

'You can say that again,' chuckled Chris.

Chris grabbed a large bottle that he had taken from the fridge and poured its gloopy contents into his, Caitlin's and Joel's glasses. Dorian held up his glass expecting to have it filled by Chris.

'It's not for you,' Chris told him coldly. 'It's especially for us and for us only.'

'What's so special about it?' asked Dorian, intrigued.

'Can't tell you that,' mumbled Joel through a mouthful of pasta. 'It's a secret recipe – passed down from our parents. It's a smoothie with a twist.'

'Yeah? What's the twist?' asked Dorian.

'Like I said – it's a secret. And it reminds us of our mum and dad. It's *our* drink. No one else is allowed it.' He pushed a jug of water across the table. 'The water's good – nice and cold. Have that.'

'Okay,' said Dorian as he poured himself some water. 'It's a family thing. I respect that. So,' he continued. 'Who's going to tell me first why they like to sleep so much?'

Joel and Chris stopped chewing when they heard the question and then threw each other a look. Caitlin kept on eating but looked across the table at Dorian, who was eagerly waiting for the first one to speak.

'Why would you ask that?' Joel asked.

'Oh, don't be surprised, Joel - your uncle and aunt told me,' Dorian answered. 'It's usually the main reason people call me in the first place. I specialise in working with children who sleep a lot. I try to find out why that is and help them to want to stay awake rather than go to sleep.'

Joel looked down at his almost empty plate and pushed a piece of pasta around with his fork.

'So?' Dorian repeated. 'Why do you all prefer sleeping than being awake?'

Chris took a quick swig of his drink then spoke first. 'Because we have really good dreams, and in mine I get to be a really famous knight and get to play tricks on people – it's cool.'

He shoved another forkful of chicken into his mouth.

'Wow - that sounds like fun, Chris.'

'It ish!' he mumbled.

Dorian looked at Caitlin who was loading up her fork with pasta.

'Caitlin? Do you like to dream too?'

She nodded.

'And what do you dream about?'

Caitlin cleared her mouth and looking almost embarrassed as she spoke quietly. 'In my dreams I'm a giant fairy who looks after everyone in Fairyland and keeps them safe from the goblins.'

Chris smirked.

'Yeah, right. Those goblins must be a bunch of wimps to fear a little girl like you. You're scared of your own reflection in a mirror.'

Caitlin's head dropped low, and her chin nearly touched her plate. A solitary tear gathered in the corner of her left eye.

'Leave her alone, Chris,' Joel said crossly, whacking him in his arm.

'Hey!' Chris shouted back.

'Okay, okay. That's enough,' Dorian interrupted, raising his arms. Chris went back to his food as Joel put his knife and fork together on his empty plate. 'Well, Caitlin, you must have to be very brave to look after all those other fairies.'

'I guess so,' she whispered.

'And you, Joel. What do you dream about?'

Joel looked at Dorian and then back at his plate. He'd never talked to anyone about his dreams before. No-one ever asked about them. He felt slightly awkward, and like Caitlin, a little embarrassed.

'There's nothing to be worried about, Joel,' Dorian said to him. 'Everybody dreams. It would just help me to know what you dream about.' He leant forward. 'I'm not here to judge you, Joel. I'm here to help.'

Joel straightened himself in his seat, trying to avoid the question.

'He's the world's greatest spy,' Chris spat out, pieces of chicken splattering across the table.

'Shut up!' Joel barked. 'It's none of his business. He's a teacher – not a psychiatrist. He doesn't have to know everything about us.'

'Yeah, well, it was you who said we oughta try living in the real world for a change - maybe he can help us.'

'I doubt it. He's just a loser like us, with no home and no-one to care about him.'

The room went quiet for a moment after that outburst and even though Joel was feeling inwardly apologetic, he wasn't going to say so out loud.

Dorian wiped his mouth with a napkin then placed it on the table, his facial expression appearing to ignore Joel's personal attack.

'Well, it was good of you all to share. That helps. So, we have a knight who likes to play practical jokes; a giant fairy who stands up to the goblins; and a spy, whose job is to protect everyone. I see.'

Dorian stood up from the table and turned his back to the children and then he turned to face them rather quickly.

'How real are your dreams?' he asked with wide eyes.

'Very real,' answered Chris enthusiastically noticing how excited Dorian looked. 'Sometimes, it feels like I'm really part of them. Sometimes it's as if I can taste the food when I'm there.'

'Me too,' said Caitlin. 'My dreams seem to be getting longer and longer and I meet more and more people every time.' Caitlin refilled her glass with more smoothie and took a long drink.

'And me,' added Joel, happier to say more now that Caitlin and Chris had spoken. 'Recently, it's been getting harder and harder to wake up though, as if I'd rather stay there – in my dreams. It's as if I have more of a life there than I do here.'

'Yeah,' said Chris sadly. 'The past few days I've had to shake him awake he's been so out of it.'

Caitlin's big brown eyes stared at her big brother.

Dorian sat down again, slowly, and looked at Joel, Chris, and Caitlin, individually. He had heard this kind of story before from other children he had taught, but never had they been so involved in their dreams like these three. He knew he had to help them. If their dreams carried on this way then it would be too late for them, just as he had said to Paul and Sue.

He knew he had to tell them, but not just yet. He needed to watch them sleep first to make sure they were the right ones. He would tell them tomorrow.

'Well, I think it's time you all went to bed – it's been a long day. Go on - off you go now. I'll clear up.'

Chris and Caitlin got up from the table saying 'thank you' for their dinner and then went off to their rooms. Joel rose from his chair and carried the dirty plates over to the dishwasher before walking to the kitchen door. He stopped and looked back at Dorian who was putting the salt cellar in its rightful place.

'I'm sorry for what I said earlier. About you not having anyone,' Joel said.

'Its fine,' said Dorian matter-of-factly. 'You're right though. I don't have anyone – not here anyway. But you do, Joel. I'm sorry your parents aren't around, and your aunt and uncle aren't what you want them to be, but you've got Chris and Caitlin to think about. They look up to you and they need you. If you give up on reality, then you'd be giving up on them too.' He paused and then turned back to the shelves. 'Goodnight.'

Joel breathed deeply. He wasn't used to someone being so direct with him – or so right. 'Goodnight' was all he could say as he left the kitchen.

Chris was already fast asleep by the time Joel entered the bedroom so he just got ready for bed too, but after hearing what Dorian had said he couldn't sleep. He lifted a photo frame from his bedside cabinet and stared at the only photograph left of his mum and dad. It was taken on their tenth wedding anniversary and Tess was smiling to the camera wearing a new necklace Adam had bought her. They looked so happy together and Joel missed them immensely.

'Where did you go?' he whispered, knowing he wouldn't get an answer to his question. He clutched the photograph to his chest, lay down on his bed and thought about his brother and sister for what seemed like hours until eventually tiredness took over, his eyes closed, and he entered his other world.

Maynard Tait

CHAPTER 7

It had just gone past eleven in the morning when Dorian decided the kids had slept long enough. He went into Caitlin's room first and stood at the end of her bed, watching her wriggling and writhing - and at one point throwing several punches into the air – completely oblivious to Dorian's presence.

Any other person would have probably laughed at the sight of Caitlin in this state, but Dorian did not. He stood with a solemn face before clapping his hands very loudly in an attempt to wake her, but she didn't react at all. She just kept on wriggling and writhing. He then shouted her name a few times, each time louder than the one before, but still she did not waken.

After having no luck with Caitlin, he left her to finish her dream before going into the boys' room and tried the same thing with them. But they didn't wake up either.

As a last resort he went to Joel's hi-fi and turned it on,

twisting the volume control until it went no further. It was so loud that Dorian had to cover his ears and the vibrations from the speakers were enough to make a clock wobble off the edge of the table it was on.

But the boys still didn't flinch.

Dorian switched off the music then threw open the curtains. Bright sunshine filled the room. He noticed Chris's eyes tighten a little but carried on mumbling to himself and dribbling on his pillow.

Dorian had worked with children with sleeping problems for several years now, but never had he come across children with such intense dreams that kept them asleep even under such extreme wake-up measures as he had just attempted.

He paced across the bedroom floor for a while then went to the window and gazed straight at the sun – his eyes not squinting once. He stood in thought for several minutes contemplating how to deal with the situation when he heard movement behind him. Joel had just woken up and was sitting up on his elbows, yawning wildly.

'Good morning,' offered Dorian.

Joel lifted a hand to block out the harsh sunlight that was shining directly at him, enough to make out Dorian standing by the window.

'Uh…yeah…morning,' he muttered.

To aid Joel's temporary loss of sight, Dorian moved in front of the sun and put Joel in a pillar of shade. Caitlin shuffled into the room a moment later, her eyelids barely open, just as Chris began to stir.

'What time is it?' Joel asked.

'It's eleven fifteen,' said Dorian.

'WHAT?' exclaimed Joel.

'Way past breakfast time. You guys really were out of it - I guess you don't normally sleep this late?'

'Er...not usually,' Chris answered. 'But I was having such a good time in my dream. It felt more real than ever before – almost too real,' he added. 'At one point I nearly got my head chopped off by the Black Knight and that's never happened before. I must've woken up just in time.'

'Mine too,' said Caitlin. 'The Queen Fairy had her crown stolen while I was playing skipping with the other fairies. I don't know how anyone got passed me, but they did. So, the Queen sent me after him and I went to look for Marshmallow Man, but I couldn't find him.' She sat down on the edge of Chris's bed and started to cry. 'I've never let the crown be stolen before and I don't know what's happened to my friend. It's all my fault.'

'Hey, hey, hey,' said Dorian as he knelt next to her, putting a comforting hand on her shoulder. 'It'll be okay – you'll find your friend, I'm sure.'

'And get the crown back?'

'And get the crown back. You'll see.'

'I hope so.'

Dorian turned to Joel who had swung his legs over the side of his bed and was staring down at the floor.

'Well, Joel,' he said. 'How was your dream? Was it more real than normal?'

'Yes. It was.'

'How?' asked Dorian, bluntly.

'I was mountain climbing. I stopped for a break, and I put my hand into my trouser pocket to get a biscuit for a snack. I still had my gloves on, so it was awkward getting it out. As I pulled it out, I also pulled out a memory stick that I'd taken from my enemy. But it fell – the whole way down into the woods below.' Joel's speech got slower and almost inaudible, as if he were embarrassed to say it. 'Nothing like that has ever happened before it my dreams. Never.'

Dorian could see that Joel was upset. 'But that's all it is, Joel – a dream, nothing more than that.'

'Yes, it is real,' barked Joel, suddenly jumping to his feet. 'It's *very* real. It's more real than this life. Can't you see? We can do whatever we want in our dreams, and it happens. If we dream it, then it comes true. If I need a fast car for a getaway, I think of one and one appears. If I need to change my clothes immediately, I think of it, and it happens.' He pointed at Chris. 'If Chris wants to put a whoopee cushion under an annoying prince, then he thinks of it, and it happens. And if Caitlin wants to be taller than all the other fairies, all she has to do is imagine it and she'll be the tallest in the land. Our dreams are how *we* want things to be. But now it seems the more we dream the more real it gets, and things are starting to go wrong. I need to get that memory stick back or everyone else will be destroyed. Caitlin has to find the Queen's crown and Chris has to stop the black knight.' Joel's face was contorted by fear and anger. 'If I don't fix the problem, it'll be my fault – everything will be my fault.'

Caitlin was crying more now than she was before and Chris sat curled up on his bed with his head resting on his knees.

Dorian walked over to Joel and put an arm around him. 'Looks like I *am* in the right place after all, Joel. But you're going to have to help me, to help you – okay?'

'What? I don't understand?' said Joel.

'You will,' replied Dorian. 'You will. Now,' he said cheerfully to lighten the mood. 'What do you say we go out and get some pancakes and waffles before a trip to the park and then you can tell me more about these fascinating dreams of yours when we get back?'

'Cool!' shouted Chris.

'Yes, please!' said Caitlin, snuffling through a tissue.

'Sure,' Joel answered. 'It'd be nice to do something new.'

'What! You mean you've never been to the park?' asked Dorian in surprise.

'Nope - or had pancakes and waffles.'

'Well in that case,' said Dorian marching towards the door. 'We'd better have double servings to make up for lost time.'

'Wicked!' they all shouted.

***

After only a short time in their company it was easy for Dorian to see that Joel, Chris and Caitlin had been deprived of so many things that should be part of a normal child's life, like trips to the museum or the cinema; going to the park or playground; meals out; sleepovers; shopping. So, once they had all eaten their fill of waffles and pancakes Dorian decided that instead of spending the day with their noses in books, he would treat them to a full day in London to help them see that there is more to life than what they've been used to. He took them to the Natural History Museum where Chris was fascinated by the dinosaurs and stuffed animals; then next door to the Science Museum where Joel spent forty minutes looking around an exhibition of old aircraft and jet planes.

Caitlin sat on the toy department floor of Harrods for a whole hour playing 'house' with loads of cuddly toys without noticing all the other children and parents milling around her. She had never seen such a place and she was thrilled when Dorian bought her a fairy costume – something she had always wanted, but had never been given, even by Paul and Sue.

He bought Chris a pop-up book about King Arthur and the Knights of the Round Table and a wooden sword and shield set, and for Joel he bought a pair of walkie-talkies and spy pen and notebook.

He purposely bought things that related to each of their dreams to show them that they could enjoy themselves in the real world instead of having to rely on happiness in their dream worlds.

***

The grandfather clock in the hall was chiming eight o'clock as they all piled in through the front door to find Paul and Sue putting on their overcoats, standing next to two suitcases.

'Oh, there you are, Dorian,' said Sue, completely ignoring the children and applying lipstick as she looked in a mirror. 'Sorry to spring this on you, but *Baby Barf* doll hasn't been selling in the United States as well as expected, so I've got to go to Los Angeles and see how I can turn things around with a new TV campaign. I'll only be gone a few days.'

'And I've got to go to New York,' said George. 'Phil Fluffmann's TV spot on TTFN has been brought forward and I have to help him rewrite the script for his video shoot.' He picked up his suitcase and bumped his way to the front door. 'Then I'm off up to Canada for a few days – I'll be back in a week or so depending on the snow, of course.' A car horn beeped. 'Come on, darling – our taxi is here.'

Sue grabbed the handle of her suitcase and pulled it to the front door. 'Our numbers are on the fridge door if you need to call us, but if in doubt call my mother first – her number should be in the address book under 'M' for mother.'

'Sue! Hurry up,' Paul shouted from outside.

'I'm coming!' she snapped back. 'Okay, bye everyone – see you soon.' Sue threw her left hand up over her shoulder as she wheeled her suitcase out the door and then closed it behind her with a bang.

Dorian stood motionless with his mouth ajar for a few seconds before noticing the dejected looks on the children's faces.

'Well, she did wave 'goodbye' – sort off,' he said. But their sad faces remained as they all made their way to the living room, dropping their bulging bags of shopping on the floor as they went and then dumped themselves on the sofas.

Dorian followed them into the room and sat down opposite them in a large, seemingly unused leather armchair.

'I guess you're used to that,' he said quietly, referring to their aunt and uncle's abrupt departure.

'Yes, we are,' answered Joel sadly. 'That's the way it's been for as long as I can remember.'

'I'm sorry,' said Dorian, worried that what had been a wonderful day was about to end in the usual way as any other day for Joel, Chris, and Caitlin.

'Now do you understand why we like to dream?' Joel continued, tilting his head towards the door. 'They don't care about us. We're just an inconvenience to them. At least in our dreams we can meet whoever we want and we're happy. That's why we'd rather sleep than wake up here. They'd rather we didn't even exist'.

Dorian leant forward and put his hands together under his chin - a deep, solemn look on his face. 'Yes, Joel, I understand. But I must warn you, if your dreams continue as they are you may find that they become your reality.'

Chris snorted a half-laugh; not sure what Dorian was on talking about. 'What do you mean become our reality?' he asked. 'We always wake up eventually.'

'Yeah,' agreed Joel. 'We know they're dreams. We know we'll still wake up and have to face our real lives here.'

'Not necessarily. You said yourselves that you're all finding it harder and harder to wake up and that your dreams are becoming more and more vivid.' Dorian stood to his feet and walked behind his chair and put both hands firmly on the back of it. 'Only this morning you all told me how things in your dreams were changing, how things were happening that you weren't expecting. If you're not careful, you might not wake up at all and you'll be stuck in your dream worlds.'

'Maybe,' said Joel firmly. 'But at least we feel more alive there. We can be somebody. Here we're nobodies. So what if they became real? Then we'd be the people we want to be. What's so wrong with that? I'd love it to become real.' Joel rose to his feet and waved his arms around to emphasize his point. 'Because then I wouldn't have to wake up in this horrible existence living with people who don't care, and I wouldn't have to feel responsible for everything and everyone.'

As soon as he stopped speaking, he dropped his head so that his chin rested on his chest. He had to try hard to stop himself from crying. Chris looked up at Joel, an immense feeling of both sadness and anger welling up in him, but he couldn't say anything.

Caitlin sat up and took hold of Joel's right hand. 'I don't want it to become real,' she said.

'Why not?' asked Joel.

She stood up beside him then looked at Chris. 'Because I care - and I wouldn't be with you two. And I get scared when I'm not with you, even if I am a giant fairy in my dreams. And one day our real parents are going to come home and then we'll be a proper family. And if I stay in my dream world, I might miss them, and I don't want that to happen.'

Joel let a tear fall down his cheek. He knelt on the floor in front of Caitlin, still holding her hand.

'That's not going to happen, Caitlin. Mum and Dad aren't coming back. That's just a dream too. But Chris and I are always going to be around for you, don't you worry. I've promised I won't leave you behind again and I mean it.'

Joel gave his little sister a tight squeeze.

Dorian had heard and learnt enough about Joel, Chris, and Caitlin to know that now was the right time to tell them. He asked them all to sit down again as he, himself, sat back down in the armchair.

'I've only been with you two days, but I think it's time to tell you a story. Now this isn't just any ordinary story, but one that only children with a special gift should hear.'

'Special gift? What special gift?' asked Joel.

Dorian leant forward in his chair, his eyes roaming from Chris to Caitlin then to Joel.

'Dream weaving,' he slowly answered.

'Dream weaving?' Joel repeated, unsure if he had heard Dorian correctly.

'Yes, Joel. Dream weaving. I believe you have this special gift although I do not and so I will tell you this story – of Alfrek the Night Mayor. This story is a warning, so listen carefully to what I have to say, because your lives may just depend on it.'

Dreamers

PART TWO

Maynard Tait

CHAPTER 8

Alfrek was the first child to be born to Prince Heldrek of Sallowell and his wife, Princess Leena. They were blessed with another son, Dorian, who was two years younger than Alfrek. The boys were best friends during childhood, and they grew into fine young men although they were very different from each other in many ways.

Alfrek was taller, stronger and had a rugged complexion. He was well renowned for his amazing physical prowess especially during the annual games where he would win most events. However, speed wasn't one of his best attributes and often he would lose running races to his younger brother, Dorian.

Apart from being a faster runner, Dorian was known as the clever brother. Dorian excelled in every lesson he was taught. He was also rather handsome and charming, which made him a favourite amongst the kingdom's princesses.

Different as they were, the two brothers were inseparable – always looking out for one another and helping each other when help was needed. But as is always the case in this kind of story, something came between the two brothers and that something was in the form of a woman.

Princess Freya was the most beautiful princess in all Sallowell and was the only child born to ruling King Moldrek and Queen Selna, which made her the next heir to the throne.

Now, as Prince Heldrek and Princess Leena were best friends to the King and Queen, Alfrek and Dorian often visited the palace as they grew up and were very aware of Freya's beauty, but it was Alfrek who fell in love with her at a young age and he would often try to impress her and win her affection by showing off his strength in front of her. Even from the age of eleven Alfrek had convinced himself that he would marry Freya and become King of Sallowell.

However, as the years passed and all three grew into mature young adults, Alfrek's constant efforts to capture Freya's heart began to wane and Freya began to appreciate Dorian's humble approach to life a lot more. Dorian certainly liked Freya and their friendship certainly grew stronger through their teenage years, but he had not shown any romantic interest towards her.

This, however, only enhanced Freya's affection for him. Dorian was kind and gentle toward her and did not show-off around her like his brother did, but Freya kept her feelings to herself for fear of ruining the close bond the two men clearly shared.

It was during Alfrek's twenty-first birthday celebrations that the truth was revealed and the way it happened only made the situation worse.

Alfrek had planned to openly declare his love for Freya at the party and to ask her to marry him. It had been on his mind for several months and as the time for the party drew closer the idea of him becoming the future king also began to take hold more than the thought of having Freya as his queen.

The evening of the party came, and it was well attended as one would expect when the King and Queen had been invited. Not only did the whole royal family attend, but so did all of Prince Heldrek's family; their servants and their families; as well as neighbouring clan princes and princesses.

The castle was lit beautifully with lanterns at every turn and the central courtyard was decorated with many species of colourful flowers. The focal point of the courtyard was an ornate pond with statues in the middle of two figures in an embrace, their right hands clasped tightly together, bound for eternity. Tables strewn with enormous amounts of food encircled the inner courtyard and a merry band of musicians played joyfully encouraging all those present to get up and dance.

The party was in full swing and then the time came for Princess Freya to choose her dancing partner. It had been a tradition in Sallowell for as long as anyone could remember that a King's daughter should commence the dancing at any party she attended, with the man of her choosing. But to choose her partner, and to avoid the chance of picking a favourite, the princess had to be blindfolded, twirled around three times in the centre of a large circle of potential partners, and whoever her outstretched hand should point to as she came to a stop would be her dancing partner. While the princess is turning, however, all the male suitors can swap places with each other hoping to get into the right place. On this occasion Princess Freya's hand pointed towards Dorian, just after he and Alfrek had swapped positions for one final time.

Although Alfrek smiled towards his brother as he stepped to take Freya's hand, his gritted teeth and clenched fists told his true feelings. He had hoped that he would be chosen to dance with the princess so that he could use the opportunity to propose. He had missed his chance.

Alfrek, Dorian and Freya may have grown up together and spent lots of time together, but there had never been a time when hands had ever been held, let alone a kiss been shared. Alfrek looked at Freya as her blindfold was removed from her eyes and he could see the delight on her face when she saw Dorian stand before her, bowing in front of her as a trained gentleman should, before the two of them joined hands for the first time in their lives. At that moment, Alfrek was surprised at the sudden feeling of jealousy and anger he now felt towards his younger brother.

Dorian too was surprised at the strange feeling he felt in his heart as he held Freya's hand for the very first time while the music started, and the watching audience went quiet. Their eyes locked together as they moved across the dance floor as if in a trance. He had danced with many a princess and courtier in his time, but never had he felt like this and never, at any time before, had he felt this way about Freya.

Freya, who certainly had feelings for Dorian, was pleasantly surprised too when she took in how Dorian gazed at her.

'Does he love me, as I believe I love him?' she thought to herself.

'Am I in love with her as I think she is with me?' Dorian thought to himself.

The pair danced for several minutes without taking their eyes off each other. As the music came to an end the enraptured audience clapped and wolf-whistled to indicate their pleasure of having watched such a wonderful dance.

Dorian, being the gentleman he was, raised Freya's right hand to his lips and kissed the back of it. As he lifted his head, he took a step closer towards her and his eyes fell on her lips and he said, 'If you'll permit me?'

Freya's heart skipped a beat and she immediately replied, 'I permit it,' before closing her eyes in anticipation.

In front of everyone Dorian kissed Princess Freya and suddenly the crowd went into a clapping and cheering frenzy. The King and Queen of Sallowell clapped too, very heartily, making their approval obvious.

Only one person did not join in the merriment that evening – Alfrek.

***

Within the space of a week the royal wedding between Princess Freya and Prince Dorian had been announced. On that same evening as Dorian ate dinner with his parents in celebration, Alfrek burst into the dining hall in a drunken stupor.

Prince Heldrek stood up, dropping his knife and fork onto his plate.

'Alfrek,' he shouted. 'What is wrong with you?'

'Wrong with me?' Alfrek yelled. 'I'll tell you what's wrong with me. Freya was to be my wife and I was to be the next King of Sallowell. I was going to propose at the party. But my little brother, Prince Dorian, has taken it all away from me.' He stumbled toward the table and dropped both fists onto it, with a loud thud.

'WHY?' he bellowed. 'I loved her, and I would have made her love me.'

Dorian stood to his feet, shocked by his brother's fury and behaviour, but answered him with the respect that he had always shown him.

'My brother, I... I had no idea. I... I wasn't sure how I felt about Freya until I touched her hand for the very first time. But if the truth be known, I have always loved her. She's all I ever think about when I'm not with her. Even at night, she's always in my dreams. In fact, I don't think I've ever dreamt about anyone or anything else my whole life and I don't think I ever will.'

Alfrek's eyes darkened as he heard this, and his face twisted menacingly.

'Well, brother,' Alfrek shouted angrily. 'I will see to it that you never have that dream again. You mark my words - if you marry Freya, I will destroy your dreams forever and I will become your living nightmare for as long as you shall live. I will make you suffer, brother, like you've never suffered before!'

At that moment Prince Heldrek ordered Alfrek to leave the castle and never to return until he had changed his heart. Alfrek vowed that that would never happen, and he left noisily, growling like a rabid dog at every person he passed.

Dorian dropped back onto his chair and looked forlorn at the spot where his brother had berated him, knowing that he had just lost his brother and best friend.

Maynard Tait

CHAPTER 9

The following month the royal wedding took place, and it was a wonderful spectacle. No one had seen or heard of Alfrek since the night he was ordered from the castle, so Dorian's cousin, Meldrek, stood in for him as ring bearer. It was a beautiful occasion and the whole kingdom turned out to enjoy the festivities.

But unknown to anyone Alfrek watched the whole thing dressed as a beggar among the swollen crowds. The fury raged within his chest as he watched from the back of the throne room, Dorian and Freya being pronounced husband and wife by King Moldrek.

'I *will* have my revenge,' Alfrek whispered threateningly before leaving the hall as the crowds cheered and applauded their future king and queen.

Alfrek rode for two hours into the darkest and most

inhabitable part of Dreadwood Forest. He had heard tales of a wild old woman who had been banished to the forest because of her so-called mystical powers. Magic had been outlawed in Sallowell for centuries after two people were once convicted of using magical powers to conjure up food and clothes for the poor people of the kingdom. This made the rulers of the time look useless in the sight of their people, so they had the couple cursed by the last known sorcerer and made to live eternally in plain sight of all the people but in a motionless state as a warning to all others who practised dark powers.

But occasionally someone else would come along and try and cause trouble using magic for personal gain. Anyone who was caught using their powers was banished to Dreadwood forest and forced to fend for themselves. They were kept within the boundaries of the forest by an enchantment that could only be cast by the ruling King at the time. The spell being passed down from generation to generation and known only to the reigning King.

As nobody could remember the last time anyone was last banished to the forest, Alfrek didn't even know if such a woman existed, but he had to try and find her. She was the only one he believed could help him with his plan to ruin Dorian. If this woman existed, she would give him more power than he could imagine.

It was almost midnight by the time Alfrek came to an abrupt stop in front of a small round building in what seemed to be the densest part of the forest. The full moon was barely visible through the thick foliage above, but there was just enough light to make out this odd structure that was placed in the most innocuous part of the forest. The light of a burning candle seemed to be hovering in front of a tiny window on one side of the dwelling and Alfrek could just make out the shape of a tiny door to the right of it.

He approached the window slowly and quietly not knowing what he would find inside. As he reached the small window he stood on a dry twig and without warning, the tiny door burst open and with great speed a dark figure appeared in front of him, and he suddenly found himself being dragged by his heels upside down and hanging in mid-air with his head several feet above the ground.

Slightly dazed but unhurt, Alfrek noticed the dark figure silhouetted against the light coming from inside the building.

'Who are you?' asked the figure hurriedly in a deep, gruff voice.

Alfrek couldn't make out from the figure's appearance or voice if it were a man or a woman speaking.

'My name is Prince Alfrek of Sallowell. I'm searching for an old woman who I believe has magical powers. Do you know of such a woman?'

'Might do,' replied the figure cynically.

'Well, can you direct me to her?' Alfrek continued.

'Maybe,' said the figure as it took a few steps towards Alfrek.

'What can I give you for this information?' Alfrek offered.

'Er...um...oh, I know. How 'bout a big sloppy kiss,' said the figure as it lit a candle right in front of them revealing the most hideous, warty, greasy, wrinkled old face with lips pouted and eyelids fluttering.

Alfrek reacted as if he'd just seen his worst nightmare and wriggled his body in a vain attempt to release himself from his bindings.

'I'll take that as a 'no' then, shall I?' said the old woman disappointingly as she took out a knife and cut the rope that was holding Alfrek up, causing him to crash heavily to the ground. 'I guess me looks have gone a bit since I've bin in 'ere. Oh well, can't blame a girl for tryin', eh? Fancy a brew – kettle's about to blow?'

The old woman turned around and went inside as Alfrek slowly lifted himself up onto his feet, brushing his clothes off with only one thing on his mind and it was not a cup of tea. He strode in through the tiny doorway and reached out with both hands to grab the old woman by the throat from behind, but as he got to within a foot of her, Alfrek's arms seemed to flop downwards as if they had just had their bones removed. He quickly jumped back, and his arms went back to normal. He flexed both his hands – they were normal. He stepped forward and tried again to strangle the old woman, but again his arms fell to his sides.

'There's no point in trying to harm me, sweetie, you won't be able to. I'm enchanted with a self-defence charm, y' see. Now sit down over there,' said the old woman, pointing to a tiny three-legged stool beside a bubbling cauldron which was floating above a roaring fire. 'An' tell me all your troubles. I ain't 'ad a visitor 'ere for over forty years, so it'll be nice to 'ave a little chat and a gossip. Mind you I ain't got much gossip,' she cackled, showing Alfrek her lack of dental hygiene.

She handed Alfrek a steaming cup of tea which he took reluctantly. For all he knew he was about to drink poison or something that would turn him into a rat. The old woman sensed his concern.

'S'okay. It's not poison, and it won't turn you into a rat,' she laughed.

Alfrek sniffed at the hot liquid and was pleasantly surprised that it did indeed smell of tea.

'Best brew for miles,' said the old woman. 'Actually, it's the only brew for miles.'

She began to cackle again, ending her fit of hysterics with an undignified burp and a potent aroma that reminded Alfrek of rotten eggs. 'Oops, better out than in,' she said as she wafted the smell away. 'Then again, maybe not.'

Alfrek stared at this frail bodied, but sharp-minded old hag with suspicious eyes. The tales he heard were of a wise old woman who could bring down castle walls at the click of her fingers; bring skeletons back to life at the wink of an eye; and summon winged serpents to destroy villages at the stamp of her feet. The woman who sat in front of him reminded him of a washer woman who'd spent more time washing clothes than washing herself. She looked harmless enough, but Alfrek knew that if this were the woman he was looking for then he would have to be careful in case she took her anger out on him for being banished to the forest all those years ago.

'So,' he said softly. 'Are you the powerful magic woman I seek?'

'Me?' she said pointing at herself.

'Yes,' said Alfrek. 'Are you the mighty sorceress of Dreadwood Forest whom all Sallowell fears? The one who can call on the evil beasts of the ground and air. The one who can bring down hail from the sky on even the hottest day. The one who can cause kings to fall at your feet?'

The old woman looked deep into Alfrek's eyes, stood up as tall as she could, then burst out laughing. She laughed so hard she had to hold her left side she was so sure it was going to split.

'Me? Ha, ha, ha. A sorceress? Hee, hee, hee.' She continued laughing, just taking in enough air to talk. 'Is that what they say about me? Ho, ho, hee, hee, ha, ha. Oh stop, please, stop. You're killing me.'

Alfrek sat with his mouth agape and watched as the woman fell onto the floor, her laughter increasing in volume as she landed on her knees.

'Summon beasts, tee, hee. Kings at my feet, ho, ho, ho. Oh, dearie-me. Am I her? Absolutely not, sweetheart. But I like the idea of it.'

Alfrek stood up fast. 'But you are enchanted. You…you caught me in a trap. My arms. No ordinary old woman can do these things.'

The old woman grabbed hold of the edge of a table and pulled herself back onto her chair as the laughter subsided.

'I've lived in the forest for years, darlin' – course I can build a trap. Anyone can do that.'

'But the enchantment.'

'Ah, well,' said the old woman. 'That's taken years of practice and thanks to this.' She tapped her hand on a book which lay open on the table. 'It used to belong to 'er.' She pointed to a skeleton that sat on a chair in the corner of the room. Alfrek hadn't noticed it as it was covered in cobwebs and a rug covered its legs. 'She was like that when I found this place and this book of spells was lying open on the table just as it is now. I keep 'er where she is for company, y'see. I'd go barmy if I didn't have someone to talk to. As for the spells, well, the protection enchantment is only one of a few that I've managed to master over the years, an' seeing as I ain't had a visitor for years, y'can see how pointless that's been – at least until now, of course,' she added bitterly, pointing a crusty finger at Alfrek.

Alfrek's anger began to dissolve as he took it all in.

'Do you mean to tell me, that you possess no magic?'

'Nah. Not really, but I can turn a rabbit into a mouth-watering casserole if you fancy it. It'll only take a couple of hours.'

Alfrek turned and made his way to the door.

''Ere! Where you goin', sweetie?' called the old woman.

'I need to carry on my search for the sorceress. She must be somewhere in this forest.'

'There is no-one else in the forest. It's just me and fluffy, tasty bunny rabbits. Believe me, I'm the only person in this place, my lovely. You're the first human bein' I've seen in years.'

Alfrek stopped and rested his head on the doorframe. 'But if you're not a powerful magician, then why are you here?

Only people with dark powers are banished and confined to the forest. And why do people fear you so.'

'Well, when I was young, I used to work as a scullery maid in the king's palace. One day the chief cook, who didn't like me very much, told me to go into the cellar and find a certain recipe book. She wanted to cook something extraordinary for the king's birthday banquet and the recipe was in a book she hadn't used for years, but knew it was in the cellar. So, I looked and looked until I found it at the bottom of a pile of books. Inside was a bookmark which had something written on it in a language I couldn't understand. I read it and read it as I walked back to the kitchens. It was only as I entered the kitchen and handed the recipe book to the cook, I read the writing correctly and suddenly there was a puff of smoke and cook turned into a vulture. And right in front of all the other servants. I was brought before the king and was made to turn the cook back again, but of course I couldn't. The king said my refusal to switch her back again only proved how much I hated her and wanted her to remain a vulture and confirmed I was a witch, so I was banished to the forest. It took me three months of wandering and sleeping under leaves before I found this place and as many years before I could make any of the spells work properly. So, nope – I ain't a magician, sorceress or a witch. I can only assume her over there,' she said pointing at the skeleton 'was the dreaded sorceress. But all the power in the world couldn't even stop her from popping 'er clogs. Now, how about a little pick-me-up, eh? Looks like you could do wiv somethin' a bit stronger than a cuppa tea.'

Alfrek plonked himself back down onto the tiny stool and

watched as the old woman opened a large cabinet on the other side of the fireplace and take out a bottle from the vast array that filled every shelf. There were large bottles, small bottles, clear bottles, dark bottles, bottles with corks, bottles with stops, and they all seemed to be filled with various colours of liquids.

The old woman turned to Alfrek. 'So, what's your poison?'

Alfrek stood again, ignoring the old hag's question; his stare fixed on the array of bottles before him.

'What are they?' he asked, motioning to the contents of the cabinet.'

'These? These are potions, sweetheart. Oh, didn't I tell you. I may not be a magician, but I sure know 'ow to make a mean potion that'll do whatever you want - well, most of the time.'

Alfrek's deep brow returned, and the evilest smile covered his broad face. He had found a way to ruin his brother after all.

'In that case,' he muttered sinisterly. 'Bottoms up!'

Maynard Tait

CHAPTER 10

Dorian and Freya were so exhausted from the day's excitement and partying that as soon as their heads hit their pillows, they both fell fast asleep. Three days of feasting and celebrating followed the wedding day and this was the first night they spent on their honeymoon.

They were staying in the palace's summer garden chalet, as is customary after a royal wedding. The huge garden is surrounded by a twelve-foot-high wall and only has one entrance. The inner perimeter of the garden has dozens of rose beds. Inside the rose beds is a large privet hedge maze. Within the maze is a small copse of oak trees and in the middle of the copse is the chalet itself. So, the newlyweds were completely alone. Or so they believed.

Alfrek and the old woman stood behind a large redwood tree only several metres away from the entrance to the garden, waiting for the right moment to gain access through the solitary gate. They then managed to bypass two palace guards who were on sentry duty at the gate to the garden by drinking a cloaking potion. The old woman warned that it would only last for a couple of minutes, so they had to get as close to the garden as possible, avoiding lots of palace guards, before drinking it. Thankfully for Alfrek he knew where most of the guards would be positioned which made their task slightly easier than he had hoped. As soon as they had swallowed the rank mixture and their bodies seemingly vanished, the two of them crept as quickly and quietly as they could passed the guards and through the gate and then ran towards the entrance of the maze just before the potion wore off and they became fully visible again.

'I thought you said it would last at least two minutes,' Alfrek barked in a whisper. 'That was barely one minute. We could have been spotted.'

'Oh, keep your hair on,' the old woman spat back. 'We made it didn't we? P'raps I should've added more frogspawn. I always get me fluid ounces and millilitres mixed up!'

'Well how can you be certain this next potion I'm about to drink will work? How do you know it won't go wrong?' Alfrek barked.

'I don't – I've never had to make this kind of potion before,' the old woman complained. 'Funnily enough no-one's ever knocked on me door before and said to me, '*Excuse me, love, but could you make me a potion to give me the power to take people's dreams away and leave them sleeping for the rest of their lives.*' This is a new one fer me, y'know. I had to mix three different recipes together for this one, so I can't be certain it'll work, but I followed the book's instructions to the letter – I think. I guess it depends on how badly you want it to work. If anything goes wrong, I've got this 'ere reversing potion,' she said, showing Alfrek another small bottle in her other hand. 'Which will bring you back to normal whatever 'appens? I've used it loads of times.'

'Oh, I want it to work alright,' Alfrek said calmly. 'My brother has ruined my future and now I will ruin his. I'll drink this potion and go in there and steal his dreams, so that he can never dream of his new bride again or wake and look upon her beauty. He will sleep forever and a day and see nothing ever again. I will then woo Freya and make her my wife and I will become the future king of Sallowell, for that is my destiny.'

The old woman reached into a deep pocket and withdrew a small black bottle and removed a cork from its top, raising it up in front of Alfrek's face.

'Well then – sounds like you'd better knock this back, hadn't you?' she said. 'But don't blame me if it all goes a bit skew-whiff.'

'Don't worry old woman,' he replied. 'I will not harm you as I will be forever in your debt.'

The old woman quickly pulled her arm away and frowned at Alfrek.

'And you won't forget your promise?' she asked.

'No, old woman, said Alfrek convincingly. 'I promise that you will be allowed to return to the city a free woman – I give you my word. NOW GIVE ME THE BOTTLE!'

Alfrek grabbed the bottle and drank the potion down in one gulp.

Nothing happened.

The old woman looked up at Alfrek in expectation.

'Anything?' she asked hopefully.

'Nothing,' he replied crossly.

'Hmm,' she considered. 'How did it taste?'

'Like the inside of a dragon's stomach and a little bit sour.'

'Aah! I know,' said the old woman shoving a hand deep into another pocket. 'Here, take this sugar lump – that should do the trick.'

Alfrek took the sweet cube and threw it into his mouth and swallowed. Still nothing happened.

'Let's walk while we wait for it to kick in,' grumbled the old woman. 'You're a big lad – it might take a while.'

So, the two of them made their way through the twists and turns of the maze, all the while waiting for the potion to take effect.

Five minutes later, just as they had made their way through the maze and reached the oak copse, Alfrek suddenly fell to his knees grabbing his throat with both hands as he tried to scream in agony, but no sound came out. His eyes bulged out of their sockets to the point that the old woman thought they were going to pop, but they retreated into place and then turned a sickly yellow colour, the pupils blackening as they doubled in size. His skin began to creep as if it was crawling with a thousand worms. His throat began to swell, as did the rest of his body from the neck down - so much so, that by the time it had reached his toes he had grown an extra two feet in height. His hair turned jet black, and it grew down to his waist in seconds. His clothes ripped as his body's muscles increased in size; his coat and shirt falling to the ground as his chest doubled in circumference.

Alfrek's heavy gold necklace and medallion which he had worn every day since his thirteenth birthday as a sign of his princely status, burned into his chest. He tried to grab at it and pull it away from his skin, but it became a part of him, making him look like a town mayor who had outgrown his jewellery.

The old woman retreated to behind a nearby tree fearful of how Alfrek would react when the transformation was complete. Only several minutes had passed since Alfrek swallowed the potion, but he was barely recognisable as a prince of Sallowell except for the necklace which glittered by the light of the moon that was now visible. He stood to his feet and looked at himself from his feet up, his arms outstretched.

'What have you done to me, old woman?' he roared; his voice now two whole octaves lower than it was two minutes earlier.

The old woman peered out from behind the tree. 'Erm, well, there was bound to be some side-effects. I didn't exactly have time to do clinical trials, did I?'

'Come to me,' Alfrek beckoned in a much calmer voice. 'Do not be afraid – you have served me well. Please – come to me. I will not hurt you.'

The old woman slowly inched her way towards Alfrek, gazing up and down at his eight-foot frame, the skin on his bare arms still creeping. He smiled an unnatural smile to show he meant no harm.

'You have given me power to defeat my enemies, old woman - now I need to know if it works.'

Without warning Alfrek thrust out his right arm and tried to plant his enormous hand firmly around the old woman's head, but he had forgotten about the self-defence charm that surrounded her. His hand flopped towards the ground, so he withdrew his arm.

'I knew I couldn't trust you,' cried the old woman, as she backed away towards the tree. 'You used me. Well, the joke's on you, ya big ugly brute coz there ain't no potion to turn you back again. You're stuck like that for good – ha! There's no way your precious little princess is gonna want to marry a foul looking monster like you now.'

Alfrek's face contorted with rage, and he moved towards the old woman who was standing still next to the tree with the other bottle in her hand.

'The reversing potion – give it to me.'

'What! This?' said the old woman with a wry smile on her face as she lifted the bottle level with her face. 'Oh sorry, sweetie – I was lyin'. This ain't a reversing potion – it's more cloaking potion – just in case you broke your promise. Just as well I brought it.' As soon as she had said this, she drunk the potion down and immediately disappeared.

Alfrek threw both his arms out in front of him where the old woman stood, but he couldn't feel anything.

'Where are you, you old hag?' he shouted with venom. 'Turn me back or I'll kill you!'

'You'll have to find me to kill me,' laughed the old woman from somewhere within the trees. 'But that's not gonna happen. This potion will last me for hours, you giant greasy-haired sack of pus.'

'I'll get you, you witch,' screamed Alfrek.

'Toodle-oo!' shouted the old woman. 'I hope you get stuck in the maze on your way out, you smelly ole poop!'

Her voice became fainter and fainter as she continued to shout insults through the maze and Alfrek ran in and out of the oak trees in a vain hope of catching the old woman not having any idea where she was.

Several minutes passed before it dawned on Alfrek that he was now on his own. It also dawned on him as to why he was standing in the centre of the garden now looking the way he did. He could no longer hear the old woman and he noticed how still and quiet the night had become and the chalet in front of him seemed vacant, but he knew that asleep inside lay Dorian and Freya.

His fiery yellow eyes almost lit up as he remembered the reason he had undergone this hideous transformation. As he walked with purpose to the front door of the chalet, his large hairy feet left deep footprints in the soft ground.

The door opened without a creak. Alfrek stood in the threshold and scanned through the darkness looking for the door to the only bedroom. The light from his eyes made it easy for him to cross the living area without knocking into anything.

He reached the bedroom door and took its handle gently in his hand, then turned it and slowly opened the door. Inside the room a single candle burned above the bed lighting the happy couple's sleeping faces.

Alfrek's scorched heart made him want to charge at Dorian and kill him instantly, but that wouldn't give him lasting satisfaction. He wanted Dorian to suffer, not to die.

He crept across to the side of the bed and looked down on his brother. Dorian seemed to be smiling and Alfrek knew he must have been having a dream about his new wife.

'Enjoy it, brother. It'll be the last one you ever have.'

Alfrek lifted his right hand and went to place it on Dorian's forehead, but he stopped short. Something troubled him. If he removed Dorian's dreams and left him to sleep forever, then it wouldn't be Dorian who would suffer – it would be Freya. Freya would have to live her life knowing her husband could never awaken and she would still be able to dream of him as she slept. And knowing that the old woman was right by saying that there was no way that Freya would marry Alfrek now that he looked like a monster, it occurred to him that the best way to make Dorian suffer would be to have him wake up the following morning and find his bride by his side and then find that she could never waken.

'Yes!' whispered Alfrek to himself. 'You will suffer, Dorian. If I can't have her, then nor will you.'

Alfrek crept to the other side of the bed and stared at the beautiful face of the woman he loved and laid his right hand on her forehead. He took a vial of potion from his trouser pocket, opened it, and dropped the contents on her lips. Freya's eyes opened immediately and fell on Alfrek's face. But as quick as they opened, they closed, never to open again.

'I'm so sorry,' said Alfrek honestly. 'Sleep well, my love – sleep well.'

***

The morning sun made its way across Dorian's face enough to waken him. He blinked his eyes to adjust to the bright light that was now filling the room. He turned his head to his right and smiled with immense pride as he stared at Freya's motionless but exquisitely gorgeous face; her chest the only part of her body that moved to indicate that she was still alive.

Dorian raised himself up onto one arm. With his other hand he caressed his wife's alabaster cheek. He then moved her hair away from her ear and he lowered himself to whisper into it.

'Good morning, my love,' he said.

Freya did not stir. He kissed her gently on the temple and then whispered the words again, but she didn't move.

Dorian sighed, but did not think anything more than that she was clearly still exhausted from the day before, so he got out of bed and shuffled his way into the bathroom. He poured some water into the sink then splashed it onto his face to make him more awake. He grabbed a towel that sat next to the sink and proceeded to dry his face in front of the mirror that was on the wall above.

On the mirror were the words – SWEET DREAMS.

Dorian smiled thinking that Freya must have written it, until he remembered that he was the last to use the bathroom the night before.

Dorian's smile faded as he turned around and looked at Freya as she lay as still as a corpse on the bed. Turning back to look at the mirror Dorian recalled the last words his brother had said to him before he was ordered to leave by his father.

'*I will become your living nightmare for as long as you shall live. I will make you suffer, brother, like you've never suffered before!*'

Dorian immediately ran back into the bedroom and fell to his knees at Freya's side.

'Freya!' he shouted. 'Freya! Can you hear me? Wake up! You must wake up.'

He began to shake her by the shoulders, but she still did not react.

'Please wake up, my darling. Please. You have to wake up – you must wake up.'

Dorian began to sob as he continued to shake her, knowing that his brother had a hand in this.

After a while he acknowledged his wife's fate then he raised his tear-stained face to the ceiling and cried out from the pit of his throat the name of the person he wanted to punish.

'AAALLLFRRREEEKKKK!'

CHAPTER 11

Dorian threw the front door of the castle wide open as he marched outside to the courtyard in anger, ordering his armed guard to mount their horses. The site of Alfrek's colourful birthday party and Dorian's splendid wedding banquet was now filled with men ready for battle. His father, Prince Heldrek, ran after him, begging him not to go.

'He will pay for what he has done,' shouted Dorian.

'But you do not know what you will find in the forest, my son. It contains all manner of evil.'

At the mention of the forest, every one of the armed guards immediately stopped what they were doing - some of them mid-mount - and turned to look at Prince Dorian. He had told them to prepare for a hunt but had not mentioned where the hunt would take them. As far as everyone in Sallowell was concerned, Dreadwood Forest was a place to be left well alone.

Everyone had heard stories about strange creatures that roamed its boundaries; stories of dangerous wizards and witches who inhabited the place and cursed anyone who came within smelling distance of them.

Dorian noticed the fear on their faces and was incensed by their ignorance.

'You live in fear because of silly tales about dangerous witches and powerful sorcerers, but how many of you have actually seen proof of these fanciful tales?' The guards looked at each other, hoping at least one of them could provide some evidence. 'Not one,' cried Dorian. 'So, mount your steeds and let us ride with courage into the forest.'

'Nay! Not I,' said one of the guards. 'I will not enter the forest until I have proof that it is safe to do so.'

'Nor I,' shouted another.

'I have not known of any man who has returned from the forest alive,' declared a third.

'That is because you haven't known of *any* man that has entered it,' argued Dorian. 'My disgraced brother clearly got the power to curse your future queen from somewhere, and that somewhere can only be Dreadwood Forest - if the tales are true. It is also the only place close to the city for someone to hide, so I have no doubt that Alfrek will be found in the forest. If we can find the source of the magic, we can destroy it, after we get the curse reversed. Then we can all go to our homes as victors and show everyone that there is nothing to fear. What do you say? Do you wish to be known throughout the land as the bravest knights of the King's court or as worthless, spineless cowards?'

None of the men moved from their spot which confirmed their reluctance to join Dorian on the hunt for Alfrek despite his valiant words.

'So be it,' said Dorian as he threw himself athletically onto his horse. 'I will go alone and prove to you, once and for all, that the forest has nothing to be feared and contains nothing more than trees and old wives' tales.'

'My son,' cried Heldrek. 'Don't go – it's too dangerous!'

'I must father - for Freya's sake and the for the sanity of this kingdom.'

Dorian pulled back on his reins and his horse reared up onto its hind legs, then charged into a gallop disappearing through the castle gates. Heldrek watched as Dorian left the castle, fearing that he may never see either son ever again.

***

Dorian and his horse found the going tough as they weaved their way slowly through the dense woodland. He had left the castle at midday and as there wasn't much daylight left Dorian guessed he had been travelling through the forest for almost six hours, but it could have been longer.

His stomach began to growl due to hunger and it was the only sound he could hear in this miserable place, except for his horse's plodding feet on the hard ground below him.

The immediate anger and hatred that Dorian had initially felt earlier in the morning had subsided slightly, but he was still driven by the desire to have his new bride awake by his side and his brother, Alfrek, punished. These feelings for his brother were new to him and at times he battled with them, almost convincing himself that it was all a mistake; that Alfrek had been tricked into doing what he did. But Dorian would never forget the ferocity with which Alfrek shouted at him on the evening of his engagement. Alfrek's hatred for Dorian was real enough and only he could take the blame for what had happened to Freya. No one else.

Dorian's horse came to a sudden stop and began to sniff at the damp air around him. Dorian urged it on, but it wouldn't move.

'What is it, Barath?' whispered Dorian as he drew his dagger out of its sheath. 'What can you see?'

Dorian peered through the grim darkness that surrounded him trying to fix his eyes on anything that did not resemble a tree.

Directly ahead of him, Dorian thought he could make out the faint glimmer of a candle. Not wanting to make any unnecessary noise he dismounted and tethered Barath to the nearest branch then slowly crept his way through the trees towards the light. As he got closer to it, he could make out the shape of a small cottage and noticed that the light was indeed a candle perched on a windowsill.

Brave as he was, Dorian suddenly felt fearful of who or what lived in the cottage. Although he had grown up with the stories about the forest like everyone else in Sallowell, he had never believed them, so he was somewhat surprised to find someone living in the forest, especially this deep inside it, which gave him more reason to believe that whoever lived here had just cause to.

He lowered himself to the ground and scanned the area around the cottage in case it had been cursed or had traps set, but it was difficult to see due to the extreme darkness and he wasn't even sure of what to look for. And then it dawned on him. This couldn't be the home of a sorcerer or witch – there was no such thing. There must only be one person inside.

Alfrek.

Having convinced himself he knew who was inside the cottage, Dorian sprung to his feet and walked briskly towards a small door next to the candle; his dagger in one hand and the other one clenched tight, still trying to avoid making any noise. However, as soon as he stepped on a dry branch and felt it snap loudly underfoot, the light disappeared, the latch of the door was lifted, and the door creaked open.

Dorian froze and for a few seconds the only sound he could hear was the faint whistle made by his nostrils as he breathed in and out as slowly as he could dare.

The forest seemed to come to a complete standstill. All the trees stopped swaying and not a single leaf moved.

Perfect stillness.

Dorian stood motionless, the grip on his dagger was solid.

The darkness was overwhelming, and fear consumed him, then suddenly.

'BOO!'

The sudden cry in his right ear was enough to make him

jump forward a whole yard and land in the middle of a rope trap. His feet were swooped from under him and a second later, he was dangling upside down by his ankles, his head about five feet off the ground. He could gauge the distance thanks to the illumination that came from a freshly lit candle that was being held about an arm's length from his face. Behind the flame as his eyes adjusted to the light, he could just about make out the most hideous face he had ever seen, even with the toothless smile and fluttering eyelids.

''ello gorgeous,' cackled its voice.

'Urgh! What manner of evil are you?' spat Dorian.

'Oh, well, thanks *very* much,' replied the old woman. 'You know it wouldn' 'urt if you men tried to compliment a woman on a first date, instead of looking as if you're about to vomit all over 'er.'

Dorian looked at the unsightly figure in front of him and thought of how he could have the upper hand.

'Well…er…my good lady,' he started desperately. 'Perhaps if I could look at you the right way up, I may have a different reaction. It's possible that even the most beautiful face may seem unattractive if it were viewed upside down.'

The old woman giggled at Dorian's words and then understood exactly what he meant.

'Oh! You want me to cut you down, so you can stand in front of me, do you?'

'That would put us on an equal footing,' said Dorian.

The old woman came nose to nose with Dorian.

'Well, it ain't gonna happen, no matter how much you flatter me, you sweet-talking, sweet-talker you. See, you're the second fella that's tried flirting wi' me since recently…'

'A man was here?'

'Yes, and he didn't quite live up to my expectations, so I'm playing it cool from now on and…'

'Was he named Prince Alfrek?'

'Yeah, that was 'im. And you ain't gonna get around me with your fancy talk and full lips, and your firm looking biceps and your lovely, wavy but manly shoulder-length thick head of hair.'

The old woman put a wrinkled hand next to Dorian's head as though she was about to caress his cheek, her mouth quivering as she started to pucker her lips ready for a kiss.

'My good woman,' said Dorian. 'I am a married man. Please do not interpret my being here as anything more than honourable.'

'Forget your honour, gorgeous,' said the old woman as she tried to plant her lips on Dorians. 'Give us a kiss!'

Dorian wriggled enough to sway away from the odious old face, threw up his right arm and cut the rope with his dagger, believing that he had nothing to fear from the old woman. He fell to the ground with a thud, quickly got to his feet and pushed his dagger towards the old woman, but not too close. 'Now, enough of this charade. Where is Prince Alfrek?'

'Ooh, you are a fit one. Oh, I dunno, do I,' the old woman answered crossly, accepting the fact that she wasn't going to get kissed. 'He was gonna kill me, so I ran off. Anyway, he ain't much of a looker - unlike you - at least not anymore, heh-heh!'

'What do you mean?'

The old woman turned and headed back to the cottage.

'Oh, put your dagger away before you 'urt yourself – you seem 'armless enough. Come inside for a lovely cuppa and I'll tell you all about it. I don't get much company round 'ere see. It's nice to 'ave a chat now and again. Who are you anyway, and why're you so interested in this Prince Alfrek?'

'I'm Prince Dorian, future king of Sallowell – Alfrek's brother.'

The old woman jerked to a halt and turned to face Dorian. 'You're Dorian? But you should be…I mean…you're supposed to be…oh dear!'

'Supposed to be what?' he snapped.

'Well, asleep,' the old woman whispered. 'For all eternity.'

Dorian cocked his head to the side as he took on board what the old woman was saying then stood bolt upright, his eyes piercing into hers, his dagger ready for action.

'I think you've got some explaining to do.'

The old woman looked sheepishly at the handsome prince.

'Ahem…er…milk and sugar in your tea, sweetheart?'

***

The old woman spent the next half hour explaining everything that went on with Alfrek and how he had promised her freedom if she were to help him create a potion that would put Dorian into an eternal sleep without dreaming, and how after he had transformed into the revolting looking monster, he then turned on her to kill her. But thanks to her foresight in preparing more cloaking potion she was able to escape and return to the forest. She knew he wouldn't come after her because he now knew that he wouldn't be able to harm her because of the protection enchantment around her. And when she heard that it was now Freya who was under the potion's curse and not Dorian, she was deeply upset and angry with herself for letting Alfrek persuade her into helping him.

She pleaded on her knees for Dorian's forgiveness, and she apologised repeatedly for ruining his life. Dorian convinced her that it was not her fault and that the blame lay with Alfrek. They now needed to work out how to get Freya back and then deal with Alfrek.

'You can redeem yourself by creating a potion that will awaken Freya,' said Dorian. 'Once that is done, then you can return to the city a free woman – I give you my word.'

'If only it were that simple,' mumbled the old woman mournfully. She sat at the table and leafed through the pages of the book of spells until she reached the section on potions then pointed a crusty finger at the top of the index page. Dorian leant forward to read what it said.

CAUTION
THE COMBINATION SLEEPING POTIONS ON PAGES 652 – 659 CAN ONLY BE REVERSED BY QUALIFIED DREAM WEAVERS. PLEASE DO NOT ATTEMPT TO CREATE THESE POTIONS UNLESS YOU KNOW HOW TO LOCATE SAID DREAM WEAVERS IF REVERSAL IS LIKELY TO BE REQUIRED.

'Dream weavers?' Dorian asked. 'What are Dream Weavers?'

The old woman meanwhile had shuffled over to the bookshelf and returned to the table holding a small dusty book before tossing it onto the book of spells just as Dorian finished his question.

Dorian picked it up and read the title – THE LOST ART OF DREAM WEAVING by Hugo Thatway.

'Dream weavers were people who had a special gift that enabled them to criss-cross into other worlds to help fight against evil and were the only ones who had the power to reverse the curse of many spells, including sleeping potions,' the old woman explained. 'But there have been no Dream Weavers in Sallowell for generations. The book says that they may still exist in other worlds, but none have been seen here for as long as anyone can remember. It's possible that the last ones who left Sallowell long ago got stuck on the other side and made new lives for themselves. I'm sorry, ducky – but it looks like your princess is done for.'

'Don't say that,' Dorian shouted. 'There must be a way to find these gifted ones. I have to believe they still exist somewhere. I must look for them.' He looked deep into the old woman's eyes. 'Can you make me a potion to cross into other worlds?'

'What? Eh? I dunno…er…I've never done it before. There is one in the book, but it'd be too dangerous. You may get trapped in another dimension.'

'I have to try. If I don't even try then Freya will sleep for eternity, and I will grow old watching her. I won't let it happen. Will you help me, old woman?'

The old woman flicked the pages of the large spell book and found a recipe called 'Transcendence'. She scanned the recipe quickly to see if all the ingredients were accessible.

'Well, can you do it?' asked Dorian hurriedly.

'Ah...er...well, most of the things I've got, but I'll 'ave to go and collect some forest fruits and fungi that are required. I ate the last of the berries this morning wiv me porridge. But I think I can do it. I'll 'ave to make loads of it for you to bring wiv ya.' She turned and pointed another crusty finger in Dorian's face. 'Just promise me that you'll come back 'ere before you run out of the stuff. If you run out, I can't come and get you coz I won't know where you are.'

'I will,' replied Dorian.

The old woman pursed her lips than took a deep breath.

'Right, then - you grab an apron and I'll go and pick some fruit. This may take some time.'

The old woman opened the cottage door, grabbed a couple of candles, and headed off into the dark forest. Dorian stood in the middle of the small cottage holding a frilly pink apron wondering how this was going to turn out, but hopeful that he may have Freya back sooner than he had thought.

***

A few hours later the old woman held up a beaker full of the freshly concocted potion and offered it to a somewhat anxious Dorian. He smelt the liquid and was pleasantly surprised by its fruity aroma, although its thick and gloopy consistency and greyish colour were slightly off-putting.

'Remember,' warned the old woman. 'Let your mind follow the dimension map shown in the back of Thatway's book as you drink, and you should cross-over into whichever world you're concentrating on. At least that's what it says – whether that's what 'appens is anything matter. Who knows how many worlds are out there? Only one mouthful should be enough to make you transcend. And don't run out of the stuff or you'll never be able to come back,' she reminded him for a third time. 'The ingredients may not be found in other worlds.'

'What exactly are these strange fruits?' asked Dorian curiously.

'Best you don't know – it may turn your stomach! Just come back before you're down to your last mouthful – right?'

Dorian took hold of the beaker and gulped heavily.

'Right,' he said. 'Here goes.'

He placed the rim of the beaker to his nose, took a sniff and then a sip. Dorian immediately doubled-over and wretched, trying hard not to be sick.

'Ugh! It smells delicious but tastes revolting!' he said through gritted teeth.

'Oh, you are precious, aren't ya?' snapped the old woman. 'Pinch your nostrils, through your 'ead back and get it down your neck.'

Dorian did as she said, taking a large mouthful of the vile liquid – his eyes closed tightly, thinking this would help.

The old woman gawped at him wondering how this transcendence was going to take place. But after a full minute, nothing happened.

'Anything?' she asked.

'No. Not a thing,' Dorian replied, still wincing from the taste. 'It's so bitter.'

'Oh, silly me,' laughed the old woman. 'Not enough sugar again. Me and me measurements.' She reached into her apron pocket and pulled out a sugar lump and plopped it into the beaker. 'Swish it around a bit then take another small mouthful.'

Dorian did as he was instructed and again stood in front of the old woman, feeling nervous.

'Perhaps another lump of…'

But Dorian did not get to finish his sentence.

Suddenly, he felt his whole body being lifted off its feet and then flung around in mid-air, with all sense of gravity being lost on him. It all happened so fast he couldn't focus his eyes on anything. All colours of the spectrum flung past him at high speed and although he felt he was moving at an incredible velocity he also had the strange sensation of not moving at all. The old woman had disappeared, the cottage had gone, and he didn't feel either hot or cold. He floated aimlessly for some time, but for how long he couldn't work out. It felt like hours, but also like seconds at the same time – if indeed time existed at this precise moment and, well, time.

What was happening to him? Where was he going?

Then as quickly as it had begun, it all stopped.

There was daylight and Dorian's nostrils were filled with the scent of damp earth as he lay prostrate on the ground. Lifting his head slowly he could see that he was lying in the middle of a vast peat bog. He looked around him and noticed that this land was completely flat in every direction and there was nothing else, but peat bog.

'Not here then,' Dorian muttered to himself before taking another mouthful of the potion.

As soon as he had swallowed, he was off again. Colours spun past him. Fantastic images of various beasts he had never seen before: buildings: people: forms of transport, all went floating through his mind. He felt cold and then suddenly hot and then back to cold again.

With a sudden thud he came to rest on top of a snow-capped mountain. Feeling the cold immediately he jumped to his feet and once again scanned the horizon for any signs of life, but there wasn't any, except for a very angry-looking winged serpent type of creature that came out of nowhere and flew towards Dorian at incredible speed. Dorian fumbled for the potion and managed to swallow only a sip just as the creature bared its teeth at him inches from his face.

Dorian wasn't floating this time. He felt as though he was being catapulted through space and time like a firework. His body was forced in on itself and no matter how hard he tried he couldn't move a muscle. He was out of control. His surroundings were the colour of lava, but there was no movement. Suddenly he stopped. He could move but there was nothing to stand on and his surroundings didn't change. Then he remembered that he only had time for a sip of the potion.

'Perhaps I need more,' he thought. He took another sip and before he could put the lid back on, he was shot through time and space like an arrow from a bow. But he didn't have to wait long before he reached his next destination.

The warm fiery orange that had filled his head for the past while had become a wet and cold blue. Water lapped over his body. Standing up he found himself on a beach. Behind him he saw huts and people milling around, some of them looking towards him.

'At last - people. Time to start my search,' he whispered. Dorian pulled back his wet hair and shook off the dripping water from his clothes as he walked towards the villagers. 'I do hope their friendly.'

The people were friendly, but he only stayed in that world for a few days after finding out that no one had ever heard of any people called Dream Weavers. At least this is what he figured out, as they spoke a different language and not one that Dorian recognised. So, once again Dorian drank some potion and travelled to another dimension. His next world was full of savages who couldn't even muster up as much as a complete sentence or a decent meal, so his chances of finding anyone there even remotely clever enough to be a Dream Weaver were very slim.

Maynard Tait

CHAPTER 12

And so it went for almost seven weeks – in Dorian's time anyway. He jumped to worlds he couldn't even have imagined existed, trying to find the elusive Dream Weavers. He wouldn't stop until he found one, no matter how long it took.

But it all changed when he jumped worlds one last time and landed with a thud onto the Pantiles in Royal Tunbridge Wells, England, at one thirty in the morning on Friday 31 October 2018.

Within seconds of landing on the hard pavement outside an emptying public bar he was accidentally pushed to the ground by a drunken yob dressed in a pirate costume as he staggered out of the door onto the street. The man apologised and helped Dorian to his feet before plodding away with the rest of his mates.

It was then that Dorian noticed the beaker inside his cloak and his worst fear came about. The beaker containing the potion had smashed as he fell and the last mouthful of the magic liquid ran down the inside of his cloak, dripping onto the pavement as he stood up.

Before his last cross-over Dorian knew that this would be his last hope as he would only have enough potion to return to Sallowell. Now he was trapped, just as the old woman had warned. If only he had heeded the warning and returned to Sallowell earlier.

He now had no choice but to stay in this world and hope to find at least one Dream Weaver here.

The following day, after a rough sleep on a bench near the common, Dorian walked around this rather large village, taking in as many details as he could. This was a new world to Dorian and there was certainly a lot to take in. The people looked like him, they talked like him, and he even understood their language, but they didn't dress like him, so the following night he changed out of the clothes he had worn every day for the past few months into some clothes that had been left outside a charity shop in a plastic bag. Although Dorian didn't understand the concept of clothes hanging on railings behind a see-through mirror - the window - he did understand the word charity, so took the clothes believing that he was indeed a charitable case.

Over the next few weeks Dorian roamed the towns and villages of Kent keeping an eye out for any possible sign of a Dream Weaver. He heard many tales on his travels especially in the local pubs and churches but heard nothing about Dream

Weavers. He fed himself by pilfering food and drink from market stalls and roadside shops that left boxes of vegetables outside, feeling guilty as he did so, but having no other choice seeing as he had no way of paying for it.

He eventually managed to get a part-time job on a fruit farm, so was able to feed himself guilt free and he was offered accommodation by the farmer's wife in the form of a two-berth caravan behind one of the storage barns.

The farmer's two young children befriended Dorian and he became very fond of them. He was often asked to mind the children in the evenings, and he enjoyed nothing more than to hear them read and to listen to them making up stories.

After a while, the farmer asked if Dorian had ever considered being a teacher as he seemed very natural with the children. Dorian pondered over this for some time and asked the farmer if he knew of any place he may get some teaching practice. The farmer replied that he would let him teach his children as he could no longer afford their private school fees, so would be withdrawing them from their school at the end of the current term. This would give him plenty of practice and set him in good stead for the future.

So, after the summer season picking fruit, Dorian became a private teacher for the farmer's children. It was during this time with the farmer's children that he noticed it was the children of this world who had the most intense imaginations and who often spoke of their dreams. He wondered if a Dream Weaver did live in this world, then it was most likely to be one from their younger generation.

Reluctantly therefore, Dorian left the employ of the farmer and offered his services to other families as a private tutor in the hope of finding a gifted child, having realised that his first two pupils were not the right ones.

As the months went by Dorian became a highly skilled tutor, specifically with children who had sleep and dream issues and began to achieve a good reputation for dealing with such children.

But Dorian only had one priority in mind every time he accepted new offers of work, and that was to see if his new pupils were Dream Weavers. If after he had sorted their sleeping problems out and realised they were not the ones he sought, he would move on, and always with a glowing recommendation.

Two years on and Dorian was still stuck in this strange world with no way of getting home or saving Princess Freya unless he found a Dream Weaver, and as every day passed his hope of this ever happening diminished – until now.

Dreamers

PART THREE

Maynard Tait

CHAPTER 13

All three children stared, slack-jawed, at Dorian, each one having difficulty comprehending all that they had just heard. If what they had just heard was true, the man sitting in front of them with a ponytail, wearing a pair of ripped jeans and white t-shirt, was a time-traveller - or to be more precise – a dimension traveller. And a prince too. But who on earth would believe such a ridiculous story?

'This is,' Chris began slowly before ending with a crescendo, 'ABSOLUTELY AWESOME!'

His excitement was uncontrollable, and he sprang to his feet then proceeded to bound around the room shouting 'COOL! WICKED! SICK!' over and over again.

Caitlin laughed at him, also feeling giddy with excitement, while Joel continued to stare at Dorian not quite sure if what he had just heard was reality or a figment of his already wild imagination.

He shuffled to the edge of his seat and fixed his eyes on the floor in front of him.

'So, let me see if I understand you correctly,' he began. 'You have come from a different dimension looking for other people who you believe can cross into other dimensions through their dreams, and possess a power to wake people who have been put to sleep by a witch's potion?'

'Yes, but technically she's just an old hag not a witch,' Dorian answered.

'And you think the three of us are these Dream Weavers you talked about, and you want us to cross over into our other dimensions as we sleep, to find your sleeping princess wife, wake her up, and then wake up ourselves in our beds, back here, in our own home?'

'Yes, yes, Joel. Oh, you make it sound so simple.' replied Dorian excitedly.

At this point Chris stopped prancing around the room, sat back down next to Joel, and Caitlin ceased her giggling and sat up straight.

'You're even crazier than we are,' Joel interrupted.

'Although you will all have to dream yourselves into the same dimension, otherwise it'd be pointless – wouldn't be so simple if you were in three different places, now would it?' Dorian added with an awkward chuckle. 'And whatever you contend with in your own dreams, you will have to contend with whenever you cross over too, because they're part of your own dream worlds and they'll follow you there.'

The three children sat straight-faced and dumbstruck for at least twenty seconds after hearing all this before Chris broke the silence.

'So, you want us to fight dragons, chase nasty goblins, run from nasty spies and whatever else we come across, just to wake up Sleeping Beauty?'

'If that's what you normally get up too in your dreams, then I guess so – yes.'

'Cool!' smiled Chris excitedly. 'Is it nearly bedtime?'

'Just wait a minute,' said Joel, springing to his feet abruptly. 'This isn't just another night in our own dream worlds. This is going to be real. And how do we know we can get back? We've all been finding it harder and harder to wake up in the mornings and our dreams are becoming more and more intense. This could be dangerous. We could get stuck there.'

'Anywhere's better than this place?' muttered Chris.

'Don't be stupid, Chris. We could get hurt – or worse. Dorian, if you're right then Chris has a point. We all dream about things that can harm us. I... I don't think is a good idea. And anyway, why should we do it?'

Dorian mulled over the question.

'You're right – it is dangerous. I can't ask you to do this. It's too much for young children. You're not up to the task. You'll be afraid and...oh, what was I thinking? How selfish of me. After all this time all I was thinking of was myself and not others. Perhaps it's best this way. Alfrek can take over the country and rule it his way. It's better for Freya to sleep for eternity rather than wake up to a world ruled by evil.'

He turned away from the children, lowered his head and walked to the other side of the room giving time for the three of them to think through what he had just said.

'What does he mean we're not up the task?' said Chris crossly. 'I can take on anything. I've had plenty of practice with knights and dragons.'

'And we can't let that nasty Alfrek take over this kingdom, the way the goblins are trying to do in Fairyland,' added Caitlin. 'If I find Marshmallow Man and ask him to help me, I know we can do this, Joel.'

Joel stood his ground, his eyes burning into the back of Dorian's head.

'Come on, Joel, man up a little,' Chris teased. 'What an adventure it'll be. Don't let him think you're afraid of everything.'

'I'm not afraid,' Joel snapped back. 'I have to look after you two. You're my responsibility. If anything happens to you it'll be my fault.'

'Then you better come and look out for us then, coz I'm going.'

'Me too,' said Caitlin firmly.

Joel sighed deeply, the idea of anything bad happening to Chris and Caitlin overwhelmed him. While he feared the worst, a spark of trepidation lit within him, and he considered Dorian's words – YOU'RE NOT UP TO THE TASK.

Joel knew for once he had to face his fears and throw caution to the wind. He was up to the task, and he'd prove Dorian wrong.

'Okay,' he declared. 'Let's do this.'

As he heard these words, Dorian lifted his head slowly and a smile crossed his face. He had hoped that by making Joel think he was a failure, he could convince him to prove himself wrong – and he had. He spun around on his heels and walked towards them.

'I knew you wouldn't let me down. And the whole of Sallowell will be forever in your debt for this. You are about a do a marvellous thing. Good will defeat evil.'

He looked up at the clock on the sitting room wall. It had just turned nine o'clock. 'It is time, children – for an adventure of a lifetime. TO BED YOU GO!'

Chris and Caitlin ran off immediately, like two young children on Christmas Eve, eagerly waiting for what lay ahead, but Joel stayed where he was looking thoughtful.

'What is it, Joel?' asked Dorian.

'What about you? I mean…even if we defeat Alfrek and wake up the princess, how is she going to feel when we tell her that you're stuck here? What are we supposed to tell her?'

Dorian turned pale and the look of excitement left his face.

'I don't believe it,' he mumbled. 'Do you know, after all these years, I haven't even thought about not getting back. I've been too busy trying to find you that I'd completely forgotten that I'd be stuck in this dimension unless I have more Transcendence potion, and that's not going to happen.'

'Then tell me how to find this witch woman in the forest and I can bring some back with me,' said Joel.

'No…no…it's pointless. You will be entering my world through your dreams. I came here because of the potion – it's not the same. You can't take anything in, so in turn you can't take anything out.'

'Well, we could at least ask her for the recipe and when we come back, we can make the potion here, couldn't we?'

Dorian's hopes were raised only for a second and then dashed.

'No. Our dimensions are so different; the ingredients are likely to be different too – there is no point. Anyway, I can't let you go there - it's a dangerous and vile place. The stories of creatures that roam the forest are legendary – although I've never heard of anyone who has ever seen them. No - I can't let you go there.'

'But if you don't, then you *will* be stuck here,' said Joel. 'And Freya will be left all alone and the kingdom will probably never recover from her sadness that will rule over the whole land if she never sees you again. And the whole reason for doing this will have been lost. We may as well not go if you're going to give up before we've even left.' Joel's voice was filled with anger. He had been convinced to face his fears and now the person who had convinced him was becoming fearful.

Dorian shook his head from side to side.

'No, I won't let you do it. I forbid it.'

Joel's jaws tightened.

'You're not our guardian – we don't need your permission. If we do it, it's because we want to, not because we've been allowed to.' Joel turned and walked out of the room. 'We're about to go now,' he called over his shoulder defiantly. 'So, if you've any advice for us I suggest you follow us. Forewarned is forearmed, as they say.'

Dorian rose to his feet and crossed the living room, suddenly spurred on by Joel's newly found confidence.

'You know, we have that saying in Sallowell too!'

***

Caitlin dumped her mattress on the floor of Joel and Chris's bedroom as the boys clambered into their beds. Joel thought it would be better for the three of them to sleep near one another in case it helped to find each other in their dream world. How this was going to happen, no-one knew, as they had never come across each other in their dreams before.

Dorian told them all to focus on each other as they fell asleep.

Suddenly, Joel sat upright.

'Okay, so we think the three of us can meet each other in our dreams, but we're forgetting one crucial point. How do we get to Sallowell? We've never been there before!'

'Just follow the sinking sun. No matter where you're going – always follow the sinking sun. There you will find my father's castle.'

Then Dorian remembered something that might help. Reaching down the top of his t-shirt, he pulled out a large medallion that hung on four gold chains. The centre piece was made up of four interlocking segments each attached to one of the chains.

'Wow! That's beautiful,' cried Caitlin. 'Where did you get it?'

'It was a gift from my parents on my thirteenth birthday. It symbolises my princely status and each quarter represents a member of my family. The top half is for my father and mother – the bottom two are for my brother and me.'

Dorian took off the necklace and then separated it into four individual pieces.

'Here,' he said, handing Joel, Chris, and Caitlin a quarter each. 'Keep hold of this as you sleep. It symbolises family and unity. This is how you will be able to meet one another as you dream, and as it belongs to me hopefully it will make Sallowell part of your dreams too. And as Freya is my wife, it should lead you to her too. It has certainly kept me close to my family all these years. I hope it works for you too.'

'Thanks,' said Joel, followed by Chris and Caitlin.

'Oh, and you may find your dreams will be different than before,' said Dorian as the three of them settled down onto their pillows. 'I mean that you may not be able to do any new things just because you want to, but you should be able to do all the things you've done in your dreams in the past – so, don't try any new stunts, eh Chris?'

'Okay, I won't.'

'And be careful in the forest, Joel – remember those creatures I've talked about may actually be real?'

'I will,' Joel replied.

'And you, Miss Caitlin,' whispered Dorian into her ear. 'Keep an eye on your brothers; they may need your help.'

'I will, Dorian. And don't worry – we'll find Freya, and you *will* see her again.'

'I hope so. Sweet dreams, little one.'

'Good night.'

Dorian switched off the light and the room was consumed with darkness. He pulled the door to when suddenly Joel sat bolt upright.

'Wait, we haven't actually figured out how to get back. This could be the one time when we all stay in our dreams. We may never be able to get back,' said Joel worriedly. 'This is insane.'

Dorian turned on the light and thought about that for a moment with his head bowed low, before lifting his head and fixing an intense gaze on all three children.

'Yes, you will,' Dorian said confidently. 'Before, you all wanted to stay in your dreams, and none of you could find a good enough reason to want to come back and wake up. But now you have a reason. Each other. If this works, you will unleash power within you that you never knew you had before. You will be helping others and who knows what adventures this could bring for you in the future. And I will be here waiting on you, so I need you to come back to me. That is your reason, and that is your goal.'

The children looked at one another.

'Your right,' said Joel quietly. 'All we needed was a good

reason and helping someone who needs us is the best reason of all. I can't believe I've been so selfish.'

He reached out both his arms and placed his hands on Chris and Caitlin's shoulder.

'Whatever happens, think of each other. We can do this if we work together. Now let's go and rescue a princess.'

As Joel lay back down in his bed Dorian walked out of the bedroom and began to close the door behind him.

'Oh, and Dorian, I don't know how long we'll be,' said Joel. 'So, help yourself to anything you want from the freezer and fridge.'

'Okay, Joel – thanks.'

'Just don't drink our smoothie – there isn't much left,' Chris added. 'And we're saving that for a special occasion.'

'Okay Chris – I think it'll be safe,' grinned Dorian. 'I'll save it for you when you wake up. Goodnight guys – and good luck.'

'G'night,' they chorused.

CHAPTER 14

Joel found himself almost at the top of the rock face, as if his dream from the previous night was just continuing. He turned away from the wall of stone in front of him to check on his surroundings and everything seemed familiar, right down to the S.N.O.T. headquarters in the distance. The air was warm around him, with an unfamiliar hint of burnt charcoal filling his nostrils. He could hear a noise in the woods below him, but it was too quiet to be able to work out what it was. He wondered where Chris and Caitlin could be and how their dream worlds would collide - even if they could.

So many thoughts charged around Joel's head, mostly whether he would be able to protect his brother and sister from all the trials they were inevitably about to face. Joel suddenly became aware of the ordeal he had gotten into, and he questioned himself. Why did he give in to this ludicrous idea?

He wasn't a dream weaver – he was just a young teenager with an overactive imagination who needed to escape the mundane existence he lived because of his useless aunt and uncle.

'What have we gotten ourselves into?' he grumbled.

He didn't have to wait long to find out. Joel heard movement and looking directly below he spotted two of Professor Pratt's henchmen climbing up after him and they were moving fast, in fact they were moving at an incredible speed.

Joel flattened himself into the rock, raised both arms, his fingertips taking hold on a thin precipice.

'So, this is where it starts?' he uttered. 'Then bring it on.'

Joel pulled himself up the chalky surface like a fly on a wall, almost defying gravity. Each hand purchase he made on the rock was secure and his legs seemed to gain strength with each push they made. Within a minute the distance between Joel and his pursuers was widened and Joel believed he had nothing to fear as he spotted the top of the mountain only feet above him.

With one last push of his legs, he reached the summit of the cliff-face, both feet landing on the horizontal surface at the same time. He turned to look back down the cliff and could see the henchmen begin to struggle on the difficult terrain.

'Come on, boys – it's easy when you know how,' Joel heckled. 'Perhaps your boss should've sent a couple of real men to do his dirty work, huh?'

'Perhaps I should have.'

Joel stood rigid for a split second and then turned on his heels to find Professor Pratt standing only ten feet away with two enormous boulders of men standing either side of him, each pointing a stun gun at Joel's chest.

Joel gulped.

'It seems that every time I'm about to catch you, Agent Swift, you suddenly disappear,' said Pratt coolly as he looked around him. 'But I seem to have you cornered this time. So, if you wouldn't mind – hand over the memory stick.' Pratt held out his arm and gestured with his fingers for Joel to come forward.

Joel was indeed trapped. There was no room ahead of him past the two monstrous goons with the guns, and as he looked behind him, he noticed the two climbers had made a lot of ground and were nearly at the top of the cliff. Joel locked eyes with Pratt and reluctantly he reached to his inside pocket to take out the memory stick when he suddenly remembered that he had dropped it in his previous dream. He had no alternative. He had to get away and find the stick.

'There's always a way out, Pratt,' said Joel confidently.

'Really? Then perhaps you'd like to show me where it is this time, boy.'

Joel looked back down the cliff just as the two climbers placed their hands on the ground behind his feet.

'With pleasure,' he grinned back at Pratt, before quickly turning and diving off the cliff, plunging at break-neck speed towards the woods, hundreds of feet below.

Pratt and his men ran to the edge of the precipice and could only watch as Joel zoomed away from them.

'Not again! I'll get you, Swift,' shouted Pratt. 'You hear me – I'LL GET YOU IF IT'S THE LAST THING I DO!'

When Pratt's voice could no longer be heard Joel pulled a ripcord and a parachute unfolded above him bringing him down slowly to the ground in a small clearing, grateful for the memory of having used a parachute to escape Pratt on a previous occasion. He loosened his straps, threw off his harness and looked upwards to check that none of Pratt's men were following him down. Thankfully, they weren't.

He scanned his surroundings quickly in case Pratt had men on the ground, but there was no-one in sight. He did notice, however, large footprints that covered the clearing he now stood in. He bent down and studied them a bit closer and realised that they must have belonged to something enormous when he heard shouting behind him, and it was getting louder and louder by the second. As it got louder, he noticed the shouting turn to screaming and then to a high-pitched wail. He glanced over his right shoulder and saw Chris bursting out through the trees running across the clearing towards him.

'Run, Joel, run!' he cried.

Joel stood stunned. It had worked. Their dream worlds had collided. Chris was in his dream.

'Chris? You're...you're...in my...you're in my dream,' offered a surprised Joel.

Chris kept running towards him, his snot-green tights looking as though they'd had a row with a rabid cat.

'No, Joel, you're in mine,' Chris continued as he charged passed his older brother. 'And unless you want to become an early evening snack for what's behind me, I suggest you run!'

Joel's eyes followed Chris as he tore passed him, running faster than he'd ever seen him run before.

'We've crossed dreams,' Joel laughed to himself. 'It worked. It *really* worked.'

Joel was suddenly stirred from his thoughts by a loud whooshing sound and the crashing of trees falling. He turned to see an incredibly large, red, two-headed dragon flying low across the clearing directly towards him, its sharp teeth bared and nostrils flaring.

'Duck!' Chris shouted.

Joel fell to the ground, his face flattened into the ground. The terrifying beast flew right over him then headed to the sky before twisting around to come down for another attack, the trees on the other side of the clearing being too close together to fly through.

Joel lifted his head off the earth, and there it was – only an arm's length in front of him – the memory stick lay on the ground within reach.

Joel threw out an arm and grabbed the stick as tight as he could. He scrambled to his feet and heeded his brother's words. He ran after Chris shoving the memory stick into his jacket pocket taking care to zip it closed. He had just about caught up with him in the woods as the dragon dove down and blasted the trees behind them with a blaze of fire. The boys kept running while the dragon took to the skies again for another attack, its thunderous roar becoming more and more deafening.

'Two heads?' Joel questioned. 'One wasn't enough?'

'I thought one head was boring,' replied Chris. 'Two heads - twice the fun.'

'Twice the danger, you mean,' spat Joel.

The trees began to thin out and it was apparent to Joel that the dragon could catch them on his next approach.

'What did you do to make it so angry?' Joel shouted to Chris, who was still several feet ahead of him.

'I put itching powder on one of its newly-laid eggs,' he responded. 'There's nothing funnier than watching a dragon with an itchy butt. I must've used too much powder.'

'D'ya think?'

The boys kept running as the dragon came down low, its shadow covering them in darkness.

'There's a crevasse up ahead!' shrieked Chris.

'Just jump into it,' encouraged Joel. 'I'll catch you.'

The dragon drew deep on its lungs, ready to breathe its deadly flames.

'No way,' called Chris as he came to a sudden halt, inches from the edge of the crevasse.

'Jump!' Joel shouted; the dragon's mouths widening open.

'I can't. I can't see what's down there.'

The dragon blew hard sending two long blasts of fire from its mouths, like bullets from a gun.

'Jump!' insisted Joel, as he crashed into Chris sending the

two of them down into the crevasse. Joel held firmly onto Chris with one hand and immediately pulled on another ripcord with the other. A parachute filled the width of the crevasse as fire engulfed the walls above them. It caught onto their chute, and it disintegrated instantly, and the boys found themselves falling towards the river below them.

The dragon couldn't follow through the narrow opening, but Joel and Chris had no time to celebrate. Chris was screaming constantly. Joel focused on the running water below and thought of an inflatable raft he had used in a S.N.O.T. training exercise.

Suddenly it appeared on the water and Joel smiled just as the two of them splashed heavily into the river, inches away from the raft.

Joel was the first to the surface and he shouted Chris's name a couple of times before he appeared next to him.

'So much for the soft landing, bro,' spluttered Chris.

'Sorry,' said Joel. 'I've never missed it before.'

They swam with the slow-moving current and climbed into the raft; Joel first, dragging Chris in after him, and the two brothers slumped against each other, catching their breath, and letting the raft carry them down river to who-knows-where.

'Just tell me that's the only dragon in your dreams?' mumbled Joel.

'Who? Davina? Yeah, she's my pet dragon – she clearly couldn't take a joke. She normally laughs them off. She's never reacted like that before. I'm sure she'll be fine in an hour or two. By the way, what were you doing in the clearing?'

'Getting away from Pratt. Y'know, he's been able to find me much easier recently. I really need to get to headquarters and give them this in case Pratt does catch me.' Joel took out the memory stick from his inside pocket.

'What's on it that's so important?' asked Chris.

Joel frowned.

'The locations of all of Pratt's laboratories – or at least that's what I was told. I just know I have to keep Pratt from getting his hands on it.' He put the stick back into his pocket. 'I reckon we go find S.N.O.T. HQ, hand this to my boss to get Pratt off our backs, and then we go find Caitlin. Who knows what kind of trouble she's in right now?'

***

Caitlin soared through the air holding firmly onto Snuzzle's mane, followed by a squadron of giant bumblebees. Below, on the ground, a score of frightened goblins ran in every direction trying to confuse their attackers, doing their utmost to avoid the oversized stingers protruding from the bees' backsides.

Only one of the goblins was carrying the Queen Fairy's crown, but Caitlin couldn't figure out which one it was. She had to go to ground and round the goblins up somehow. She pulled Snuzzle's mane to the left and he turned hard and swooped down to land next to a giant frog. Caitlin jumped from one mode of transport to the other. She dug her heels into the frog's sides, and it hopped forward as though it had been fired from a cannon. It leapt after all the goblins one by one, corralling them in between four large rocks with no way out. As Caitlin motioned the frog slowly forward, the goblins all began to tremble nervously. The bees all landed in formation behind Caitlin and the frog, their stingers still ready for action.

Caitlin jumped to the ground and put her hands on her hips. She scowled at the goblins, scanning across all their faces, trying to weed out the guilty culprit. Then she spotted him.

'You!' she shouted, her right index finger pointed at a rather sheepish looking old goblin, snuggled in the middle of the pack. 'Step up front and hand it over.'

The culprit made his way out of the group rather slowly and walked, head bowed, toward Caitlin. As he reached her Caitlin crouched down. She opened her hand out to receive the stolen crown.

'You're a very naughty goblin,' scolded Caitlin. 'I ought to take you straight to the Queen Fairy and let her deal with you herself.'

'Oh, please don't do that,' squeaked the goblin. 'I'm ever so sorry. It's just that it's ever so shiny and pretty, and us goblins like shiny, pretty things. We just can't help ourselves sometimes – can we boys?'

'No!' replied his friends in unison.

'Hmm.' Caitlin considered. 'And I suppose it had nothing to do with trying to overthrow the Queen Fairy so that goblins could rule Fairyland, did it?'

'Why, no,' replied the sneaky little creature. 'Whatever gave you that idea?'

'Well, seeing as I've got the crown back and I need to find the palace of Sallowell, I'm going to let you go this time. But be warned - if I catch you again, I may not be so forgiving. I'll take this back to the Queen, and you be on your way, or I'll set Marshmallow Man on you.'

And at the mention of his name, her large pink friend appeared behind her, causing all the goblins to shake in their upturned shoes.

'And don't ever try and barbecue him again,' Caitlin roared at the frightened horde. 'Or I'll have you all locked up forever and ever.'

The moment Caitlin had fallen asleep she knew she needed to find her big, pink friend. She rallied her troops and flew to the goblins lair with the bumblebee army. She had spotted Marshmallow Man tied to stakes in the ground next to a roasting pit and an enormous bowl of melted chocolate. The goblins had tricked Marshmallow Man into following them by teasing him with a large bowl of ice-cream and it was clear they were intending to have them for pudding. She had obviously arrived just in time.

'Now leave and go beyond the border lands,' she ordered.

'Oh, thank you, thank you,' uttered the thieving goblin as he began to creep away past the bees, beckoning to his friends to follow him – all eyes transfixed on Marshmallow Man in fear. As soon as they felt they were safely out of his reach, they all turned and scurried away towards Goblin City, deeper within their domain - Snuzzle chasing them for a while to speed them on their way.

'Well, that's them taken care of for now, but they'll be back,' Caitlin said to Marshmallow Man. 'Now we'd better go and find those brothers of mine. Who knows what kind of mischief they've gotten themselves into? And you, big guy - stay close.'

Maynard Tait

CHAPTER 15

Joel and Chris yelled at the top of their voices as the raft flowed speedily through rapids, tossing the two boys to and fro as it landed on each wave. What began as a gentle float down river turned into a rollercoaster ride within seconds and neither boy had time to consider their options before being thrown around the boat.

'Do something,' Chris yelled at Joel.

'I'm trying,' Joel howled back.

'Try harder!'

In the blink of an eye the raft turned into a rowing boat.

'That's not what I was hoping for,' Chris roared.

'Me neither,' Joel responded angrily.

A second later the rowing boat changed to a canoe and

both boys were knocked around inside it; the water splashing all over them and covering the floor of the canoe.

'I don't know what's going on,' Joel shouted. 'I'm thinking of a rescue dinghy and it's not happening.'

'Concentrate!' Chris bawled as he pointed ahead of them. 'Because we're running out of time.'

Joel strained his eyes to look through the mist the choppy waters were giving off to see what Chris was pointing at.

A waterfall was coming up fast.

Joel closed his eyes and thought hard about nothing else except a rescue dinghy.

'Quickly!' Chris ordered.

The drop was only a few feet away.

Suddenly, the canoe fell away beneath them over the edge of the waterfall, and once again Joel and Chris were falling, but only for a few seconds as the hand glider they were strapped into caught onto a thermal wind and took them away from the deadly waters.

'That was close,' said Chris in relief.

'Yes, it was – I'm sorry', said Joel. 'For some reason, I couldn't transform the boat properly. I think I'm losing my powers.'

'In that case, we'd better land this thing quick. Just don't think of anything else until we reach the ground.'

Joel agreed and he spiralled the hand glider down in the direction of S.N.O.T. HQ which was now in sight.

They landed safely next to a brilliant white concrete building which stood in clear view for any passer-by to see. The large neon letters S.N.O.T. flashed from the rooftop.

'You know for a secret agency,' Chris giggled. 'This isn't very secret.'

'Yeah, well, it was so I could find it easily, and we have, so there.'

'And so will Pratt if he's still following us.'

'Okay, smart mouth,' Joel retorted. 'Look, I'll be in and out in a couple of minutes. You stay out here and keep watch in case Pratt comes along. If he does, show him a couple of tricks or something to keep him occupied.'

'Okay!' said Chris.

'Right,' said Joel, as he approached the keypad to enter the building. 'And don't do anything stupid.'

'I won't,' replied Chris coolly.

Joel punched four numbers into the keypad and a heavy door slid open. Joel went in and the door closed behind him immediately, leaving Chris standing alone outside.

The corridor was dimly lit, and Joel struggled to see much in front of him. To his right there was a glass wall. In the room on the other side of the glass, there were panels of monitors with different views of the land they had just crossed. He noticed the screen in the middle showed the front door where he had entered, and he could see Chris pacing in front of the camera and then making sudden moves as though he were fighting someone. Joel couldn't help but smile as he watched his little brother play-fighting against thin air. It was a comical sight.

Joel's moment of amusement was broken by a sharp, gruff voice, calling his name.

'Agent Swift. It's good to see you.'

It was Agent Smith. At least it sounded like him. He was a nondescript character. Tall, slender, dressed in black from head to toe. In fact, everything about him was black. It was as though Joel was staring at a three-dimensional shadow. Joel couldn't make out any facial features due to the lack of light, but it was definitely his voice.

'Er...' Joel began. 'Where's your face?'

'You never gave me one. I'm part of your dream remember. Very clever idea, Swift. To keep my identity hidden.'

'Yeah,' said Joel. 'I guess so.'

'Anyway, I'm glad you could come in, Swift – we've been expecting you for some time now. You have the memory stick?'

'Yes,' replied Joel, putting a hand into his coat pocket. 'It's right he...'

He froze. He then padded his hands over all his pockets, but to no avail. 'The memory stick – it...it's gone!'

'What do you mean 'gone', Agent Swift?' growled Agent Smith. 'If that information gets into Pratt's hands, there's no telling what he'll do. But my guess is that he'd be hot on your trail to find you and kill you.'

'It must have fallen out of my pocket when we went over the waterfall,' Joel said thoughtfully until he cottoned on to what

Agent Smith said. 'Kill me?' he screeched. 'Why would he want to kill me? If he finds the stick, then he's got what he wants and he can use the information to take over the world. Why would he want to kill *me*?'

'*Take over the world*?' questioned Agent Smith. 'He can't take over the world with what's on that stick, Agent Swift. Whatever gave you that idea?'

***

Professor Pratt's scrawny frame stood to attention after picking up the memory stick, he found on the riverbank at the foot of the waterfall. A victorious grin covered his angular face, and he lifted the stick above his head.

'Computer!' he demanded.

His henchman passed him a tablet and Pratt inserted the memory stick, licking his lips in anticipated triumph. But as quickly as the smile appeared, it vanished when Pratt's eyes fell on the screen before him. He began to snarl and grind his teeth and then he smashed the computer several times on the rock in front of him.

'BANANA MUFFINS!' he boomed heavenwards. 'IT'S A RECIPE FOR BANANA MUFFINS! I've been chasing this boy for as long as I can remember, risking life and limb, speaking in this ridiculous squeaky voice, and for what? A recipe for banana muffins. I don't believe it!'

Pratt puffed his cheeks in and out in anger then ran to all his henchmen individually, punching every one of them in the stomach, although it didn't have any effect on the muscle-bound oafs, before falling on his knees and screaming.

'Well, I've had enough. I'M GOING TO KILL YOU, AGENT SWIIIIIIIIFT!'

***

Joel tried to find Agent Smith's eyes on the visage in front of him but couldn't.

'Muffins?' he asked in disbelief. 'What have banana muffins got to do with any of this?'

'That's what's on the stick - don't you remember?' asked Smith. 'When you started this whole charade, you were clever enough to think of a way to keep Pratt from controlling this world, by making him do nothing but pursue you. You thought if he did catch you, which you said would be highly unlikely because you could escape from him at any time, then it wouldn't matter what information you put on the memory stick, as long as it wasn't something that could harm anyone – so you thought of banana muffins and put your grandmother's recipe for them on the memory stick. Only now, things have changed. You're slowing down, Agent Swift. You seem to be slowly losing your ability to transform for an unknown reason.' Agent Smith crept towards Joel and began to talk more slowly. 'And if Professor Pratt has found that stick, he isn't going to be best pleased with you when he finds out what's on it – unless he has a craving for fruit-based snacks.'

Even though Agent Smith's head was only inches away from Joel's, Joel still couldn't make out a face, but he heard every word perfectly and he began to think of how his dilemma had suddenly doubled in size. Not only was he here to help Dorian, but he also now had to escape the clutches of a crazy, evil madman who only had one thing on his mind - revenge.

He turned his back on the wall of monitors and began to take in all he had heard and to try and think of a solution.

Meanwhile, outside, Chris continued to do karate moves towards the camera thinking no-one was watching him.

***

Chris stopped his karate moves when he heard a rustle in the bushes that surrounded the front of the S.N.O.T. HQ. He took a few steps away from the building, concentrated his thoughts, and at once a sword appeared in his gauntlet covered hand, armour covering his body. Although, no helmet appeared, and his white ruff stayed in place, flopping around his neck.

'What the...' he mumbled, as he ripped off his ruff. 'Who's there?' he called out. 'I'll have you know I'm a master swordsman and I have slain many dragons, so I fear no man, woman, boy or girl.'

The bushes didn't move. After a few more seconds Chris withdrew a little, relaxed his fixed gaze on the shrubbery and he began to practise his fencing steps.

'En guard! Advance. Advance. Lunge', he said with every move.

He stepped back again.

'En guard! And advance. Advance. Parry. Parry. And riposte,' he said loudly as he thrust forward his sword.

But Chris's practise was cut short by more rustling from the bushes. This time they parted and out trotted the Black Knight sitting on his horse which was steaming from, what was clearly, a very long hard ride.

'I'm glad I found you deep in practise because you're going to need it,' said the knight as he dismounted. 'But I think you need to work on your lunge. Your short arms are no match for my long limbs.'

'Well, well, well,' said Chris. 'If it isn't Mister Poopy Pants himself.'

'That's Prince Poop to you, you little squirt,' responded the knight as he tiptoed noisily to Chris's left, dressed head to foot in full amour. 'You humiliated me at the games in front of the king and Princess Patience and I will have my revenge, once and for all.'

'Yeah, well, we'll see about that,' Chris said confidently as he matched the Black Knight's footwork. 'You may be big and ugly, but I'm small and nimble, so prepare to meet thy doom, cabbage breath.'

'And you yours, you little pimple,' the knight parried.

'Prepare to be slain, you big barf bag.'

'You tiny slop bucket.'

'You nappy sack.'

'Nappy sack?' repeated the Black Knight. 'What kind of insult is that? Enough of this nonsense. En guard!'

The knight raised his large silver sword above his helmet with both hands ready to swipe it down on Chris.

'Wait!' Chris shouted. 'I'm not ready – I need a helmet.' He thought hard and suddenly a milkmaid's bonnet covered his head. The knight laughed loudly. Chris tried again and the bonnet changed into a cowboy hat.

'What kind of magic is this?' asked the knight as he continued to laugh.

'Not very good magic,' replied Chris as he gave one last hard thought. The cowboy hat transformed to a court jester's hat, complete with three silver bells.

'Enough!' hollered the Black Knight. 'You will die as the fool you are.' And down came the heavy sword, cutting off one of the silver bells from Chris's hat, narrowly missing his right shoulder. 'Fight me, you clown.'

Chris stepped backwards and raised his sword, which he noticed was comparably shorter than that of his opponent. Another swipe from the knight clanged against Chris's sword and it took all of Chris's strength to hold onto it. He stared at the knight's sword in a separate attempt to even their weaponry. In a flash, the knight's sword halved in length. But this only made his third strike faster than the previous two as it wasn't as heavy as before. It struck Chris on his left shoulder knocking him sideways to the ground.

'You're making this too easy for me, boy. Stand up and fight like a man.'

'That wasn't meant to happen. What's going on?' wondered Chris as he sprung to his feet, but the knight attacked again, his sword thumping into the ground where Chris had fallen.

Chris skirted around the knight, thankful that he wasn't in

full armour otherwise he wouldn't be able to move around so nimbly.

In his past dreams all his battles and swordfights ended quickly, and no harm came to anyone - everyone walked away. This was different. Chris was actually feeling the pain and the consequences.

He had to do something, and quick. He ran to the front of the building and shouted into the camera that kept watch over the entrance. He shouted and gestured to try to get someone's attention but ran away just before the knight took another swing at him. Chris ran over to the bushes to give himself a few seconds. He gripped his sword in both hands and concentrated on a shield.

'Give me a shield. I need my shield. Give me my shield.'

But it didn't work. His short, but useful iron sword, turned into a balloon sword that he once had made for a friend at a birthday party. His eyes and mouth gaped open as the Black Knight approached him at speed.

Chris began to run away from the knight in a circle, trying to keep out of his reach.

Meanwhile, inside the S.N.O.T. HQ Joel came up with a plan. He knew that Pratt was going to follow him, no matter what, but he remembered what Dorian had told him about Dreadwood Forest. He had to hope that Pratt and his men knew about the forest and that they wouldn't follow him in, or if they did that the creatures Dorian had warned him about would see them off. They had to find the old woman and get to Sallowell palace as quickly as possible before they lost all their powers and woke up back in their bedroom. The quicker they moved, the further behind Pratt would be. They may have been having longer sleeps the past few nights, but they would have to wake up at some point and if they did before they reached Princess Freya then all this would have been for nothing.

Joel faced Agent Smith.

'Agent Smith, I have to leave. I'm on a mission to save a princess – I may be off coms for some time, so don't try to contact me.'

'Okay, Swift. I wish you luck, but I have to ask,' Smith said pointing at the middle monitor behind Joel. 'Is he with you? Because if he is, I reckon you could do with a new partner.'

Joel spun around to view the screens and watched as Chris ran back and forth across the camera trying to escape the Black Knight's clutches, gesturing frantically for help.

'Chris!' Joel shouted.

Chris was in trouble. His balloon sword had burst as he used it to fend off a ferocious attack from the Black Knight and he now had no weapon to defend himself. He ran once more toward the camera and yelled into it for Joel to come out and help him, unaware that Joel was on his way out.

But it was too late. Chris turned around to find the Black Knight towering over him with his sword pointed directly at Chris's chest.

'It's over, Sir Chris of Scamalot. You can't blag your way out of this one. Who's going to save the knight in shining armour now, eh?'

The black knight pulled his sword arm back ready to lunge just as a large dark shadow enveloped him.

'Well,' said Chris evenly. 'I reckon it'll be an over-sized pink marshmallow.'

'Huh?' exclaimed the Black Knight, turning around to find Caitlin fluttering her fairy wings against Marshmallow Man's nose.

'Sneeze, Pinky!' called Caitlin, dropping to the ground out of harm's way, her wings unable to keep her up any longer.

Without further warning, Marshmallow Man sneezed an almighty sneeze and a large blob of pink goo gushed out of his nose and splattered all over the Black Knight.

The gooey substance enveloped the knight and Caitlin laughed at the sight of him struggling to break free. She beckoned Chris over to her.

'Quickly,' she called. 'They always come in twos.'

Marshmallow Man sneezed again, sending another blob of sticky mess all over the knight and rendering him immobile. He stood rigid like a snowman – a muffled moan coming from his head.

Suddenly, Joel came running out.

'It's okay, Chris – I'm here.' He took a long look at Caitlin who was twice the size she normally was and then an even longer look at the moving Marshmallow Man towering over them.

'Caitlin, you're okay – weirdly huge, but okay,' he said as he hugged her waist – his head only reaching as high as her belly button. 'Where have you been, I was worried sick.'

'Oh, just kicking some goblin butt. I got the Queen Fairy's crown back, so I had to take it to her, and I told her what we were up to. She was ever so impressed, so she gave me the rest of the day off.'

'Well done, sis,' said Joel.

'Boy, you're big,' said Chris chuckling as he too threw his short arms around Caitlin. 'And I never thought I'd say this, but thanks for rescuing me. Looks like you can handle yourself after all.'

'Don't thank me,' replied Caitlin. 'Thank Pinky for being ticklish.'

'Thanks Mr Marshmallow Man,' Chris shouted up.

The three stood hugging for a bit longer before Joel broke away.

'Okay, so we're all here, but we have to get going. Pratt's on our tail and we've got to reach Dreadwood Forest before he finds us.'

'And *he* won't be stuck forever,' added Caitlin looking towards the Black Knight.

The Black Knight wobbled ever so slightly, mumbling though the pink candy, as Joel, Chris, Caitlin, and Marshmallow Man headed off at a brisk pace through the bushes in search of Dreadwood Forest.

Maynard Tait

CHAPTER 16

The hilly terrain made the walk to Dreadwood Forest a long and exhausting one, although the weather was kind to them as no rain had fallen since their arrival, which made the ground underfoot dry and firm. All the children found it strange to be in a land where the sun seemed to stay in the same position the whole time, but at least it made it easier to find places.

As they reached the edge of a plateau at the top of the highest hill they had to ascend, they were greeted by an awesome sight on the other side.

At the foot of the hill, which was covered in a layer of snow, Dreadwood Forest stretched out before them for what seemed to be miles and miles and miles, to their left and to their right. The trees were tightly packed together with no sign of life, but they had been told different – they believed this part of their journey may be the hardest and most challenging yet and possibly the most frightening, considering what Dorian had told them about the legendary creatures that lived there.

Joel looked at Chris and asked him if he was ready for the next part of their journey. Chris nodded.

Joel then turned to ask the same of Caitlin. Caitlin, however, wasn't standing as tall as she had been just moments before. She wasn't her usual fairy size at least, but she had certainly shrunk, as her shoulders were now level with Joel's head and not her waist. Her wings were barely visible too.

'Caitlin, what's happened to you? You're getting shorter.'

'I don't know - I'm a bit scared,' she replied, her stare fixed on the forest below.

Joel put an arm around Caitlin's waist. 'Look, it'll be fine. We've managed to win our battles in the past, we just have to think clearly and stay ahead of trouble. And anyway, Dorian said he doesn't know anyone who's ever seen any creatures in the forest, so for all we know there's nothing down there. I mean it certainly doesn't look inhabited, does it?'

'But those trees look humongous,' Chris chipped in. 'There could be a whole city of ferocious and deadly monsters down there. They could be watching us right now without us knowing, while they sharpen their axes and put their cauldrons on to boil, so they stew us to death with onions in our mouths.'

Caitlin grabbed Joel's hand in hers and did all she could to hold back a tear that was gathering in her right eye.

'Pack it in, Chris,' Joel scolded. 'That isn't going to help, is it? Look, as long as we stick together, we can use what little powers we've got left to defend ourselves if needs be.'

'And we've still got Pinky,' chirped Caitlin, as she looked happily up at her colossal marshmallow friend. 'You'll protect us, won't you?'

Marshmallow Man looked forlornly down at Caitlin and shook his head then pointed at the forest with a sad expression on his face.

'I think he's saying he's too big to go through the forest,' Chris said.

Marshmallow Man nodded in agreement.

'But you have to come, Pinky,' said Caitlin desperately. 'I need you with me.'

A large white tear fell from Marshmallow Man's face and splashed onto the ground like a broken snowball.

'It's alright, Caitlin. You'll have us two, won't she, Chris? We'll look after you,' said Joel kindly.

'Er, yeah. Of course – or maybe, you could keep us safe,' suggested Chris. 'I mean, look at you – you're still seven feet tall. I wouldn't mess with a seven foot eight-year-old.'

Caitlin giggled at Chris's suggestion.

'I know,' said Joel. 'What if...er...Pinky here, went around the Forest and met us at the palace on the other side. I mean, he's had to walk ever so slowly just to stay with us this far. If he walked at his own pace, he'd get around this place in no time.'

'Good idea,' agreed Chris.

'Okay,' said Caitlin. 'I guess so.'

She put a hand onto Marshmallow Man's squidgy leg and wished him well on his journey.

'We'll see you soon, Pinky. And don't worry, I'll be fine –
I'm with my brothers.'

And with that, Marshmallow Man turned and headed down
the slope towards the west side of the forest, each step leaving a
large footprint in the snow behind him.

'Right, we'd better get going – it may take us some time
getting through all this snow,' said Joel.

'Well, if we'd thought about it, we could've asked Pinky to
carry us down before sending him away,' said Caitlin exasperated.

'Er...yeah. That would've been a brilliant idea,' Chris
added, looking back across the plateau. 'Considering we've got
company. Look!'

Joel and Caitlin wheeled around to see Professor Pratt and
his men hurtling across the flat ground on ski-doos, as if they
had eagerly anticipated the snow ahead of them. Next to them
rode the Black Knight whose horse was galloping at amazing
speed, and he was followed by six other knights on equally fast
horses.

'Looks like they've got a whole heap of horsepower,' said
Joel.

'We could do with some of that ourselves, Joel. Can't you
do something,' shouted Chris infuriatingly, as the gap between
them and their rivals diminished very quickly.

'I'll try.'

Joel looked back intently at one of the ski-doos that was
racing toward him. Unexpectedly, a beat-up toboggan appeared
ahead of them, with one rail snapped in half.

'That's no use!' screamed Caitlin. 'Concentrate harder.'

'I'm trying,' Joel shouted.

He gritted his teeth, frowned heavily and suddenly the toboggan changed into a sleigh, complete with eight carrot-munching reindeer.

'Aw, come on,' Joel cried.

He tried again, this time he closed his eyes, slowed down his breathing and focused on a previous dream that he had had of a holiday in the Arctic Circle hoping it would do the trick.

'Hurry, Joel,' said Chris evenly. 'We haven't got all day.'

It worked. The reindeer and sleigh disappeared, and a shiny red skidoo took its place.

'Alright! Now that's what I'm talking about,' smiled Joel, jumping onto the front seat, Caitlin and Chris immediately leaping on the seat behind him.

Joel turned the key and pulled back on the throttle sharply. The skidoo lurched forward, and they were off. They reached the snow within seconds and the soft white powder spewed up high into the air just as their chasers flew over the edge of the plateau only yards behind them.

Once again, the chase was on.

'I knew you had it in you, bro,' Chris yelled across the roar of the engine.

The snow slowed the Black Knight and his companions right down, but Pratt's ski-doos carved their way through the snow like knives through butter and Joel had to use all his experience to keep ahead of them.

Trees started to appear quicker than expected, but Joel skilfully manoeuvred his way around them.

It wasn't enough. The weight of all three of them was stopping their transport from going as fast as it could, and Pratt's henchmen were gaining on them. The edge of the forest was close, but not close enough.

'Chris,' Joel hollered over his shoulder. 'It's your turn to do something – I'm out of transfigurations. You need to give us some time.'

'I'll try,' Chris responded worryingly.

He squinted his eyes shut and in no time at all a shower of blown-up whoopee cushions fell on the snow behind them. Their attackers rode over them with ease, albeit making farting noises as they flattened on contact – the sound echoing off the snow and trees around them.

'Now's not the time for fart jokes, Chris,' screamed Caitlin.

'Okay, I need to try something else,' said Chris thoughtfully. 'I know. I'll use my birthday party popper. That'll stop 'em.'

Chris concentrated so hard that his cheeks turned bright purple.

Pratt was catching them fast, however, his gleeful grin fell from his face as he wondered why Chris was pointing at him. He didn't have long to wait to find out.

Chris threw a length of string over Caitlin's shoulder in front of him and told her to tug on it sharply whenever he shouted 'Pull'.

On Chris's right shoulder was an enormous party popper and he gripped it tightly with both arms wrapped around it.

He aimed it at Pratt who was on the closest skidoo; closed one eye and warned Caitlin and Joel about the big bang. And then he shouted.

'Pull!'

BANG!

The force of the blast sent Joel, Caitlin and Chris flying forward as if they were gliding across ice.

The contents of the party popper burst out behind them, and thousands of streamers floated across the faces and helmets of their hunters causing some of them to crash into trees and some into each other. Pratt, however, thudded into a snow-covered boulder and he was thrown off his skidoo, landing headfirst in the snow, his legs flapping uncontrollably in the air.

The Black Knight and his cohorts reached Pratt and his men just as Joel steered his skidoo straight into the darkness of Dreadwood Forest.

They had made it.

Pratt pulled his head out of the snow and screamed an ugly scream.

'AAAAGGGHH! I nearly had you that time, Swift – I'm not done with you yet.'

The Black Knight trotted over beside him.

'The tales of Dreadwood Forest are enough to make a man insane just by listening to them. They won't get far in there – the devilish creatures will finish them off. But if they don't, we'll be waiting for them. We can ride to the east and go around the forest and wait for them on the other side.'

'But we'd have to go through Goblin Domain,' warned Pratt.

'So be it,' said the Black Knight defiantly. 'I've a feeling they'd be more than happy to join us in our pursuit.'

CHAPTER 17

Although the sun was still in the sky above the forest, it felt as though it didn't exist inside it. The darkness was overwhelming, and the closeness of the trees was too much for the skidoo, so the three explorers had to abandon it and make their way on foot in search of the old woman's cottage. And as they had no sun to follow, it wasn't going to be easy. They had only been walking for about thirty minutes when Joel told them to stop and rest.

'It feels like we're going round circles already,' moaned Chris.

'And my feet hurt,' complained Caitlin softly as she went to sit down on a log.

'Wait,' said Joel. He stepped over the log to stand next to Caitlin; her head only reaching as high as his chest. She had shrunk again – quite considerably. She was now no bigger than her normal self and her wings had completely vanished. Caitlin dumped herself down on the log and put her head on her knees.

Chris tried to do a trick or think of a silly prank to cheer her up, but he was unable to.

'What we need is heat and something to drink,' said Joel.

He tried to conjure up a warm fire and a flask of hot chocolate, but nothing appeared.

'We're just as useless here as we are back home,' mumbled Caitlin through her arms and she began to sob.

'No, we're not. We are who we make ourselves,' Joel injected. 'We have to believe we're as good as we think we are in our dreams, and we'll be fine. You can't give up now – we've still got a job to do. We can do this. Right, Chris?'

'Sure,' he replied brightly. 'If we don't believe in ourselves, then we're done for. We have to accept whatever comes our way and deal with it head on, just as we are.'

Joel stared at Chris as though he had just made his inaugural speech as President of Dreamland.

'That's very profound.'

Chris walked past Joel giving him a pat on the back.

'I learnt from the best.'

Joel smiled and then took Caitlin's hands in his.

'Do you remember what Dorian said to you when we first met him – about bringing your inside out?'

She nodded.

'Well, you may not really be eight feet tall or fly like a bird, but the Caitlin in your dreams is part of the real Caitlin. How you make yourself in your dreams can be reality if you let it. You just have to believe in yourself. And I believe in you. Sometimes we have to put our trust in other people and let go of our comfort blankets.'

'You mean, like Pinky,' Caitlin asked.

'Yes, like Pinky. He'll be there when you want him, but he doesn't have to be there when you need him, coz you can do it yourself. And who's the Fairy Enforcer anyway?'

'I am,' answered Caitlin, lifting her eyes to meet her brothers.

'And who got the Queen Fairy's crown back and delivered it to her in person?'

'I did, but that's when I had wings and was twice my height.'

'But it was still you. You did it. Now are we going to rescue this princess or are we going to let her sleep for eternity and leave Dorian back at home?'

'We're going to rescue her,' Caitlin said positively.

'And who's going to kick Alfrek's butt?'

'I am,' Caitlin shouted.

'Ata girl,' Joel said as he gave his sister a tight hug.

'Shh!'

It was Chris.

'Something moved up ahead,' he whispered. 'I couldn't see what it was; only that whatever it was it had horns.'

Caitlin squeezed Joel hard again.

'It's okay!' he reassured her. 'You can do this.'

Caitlin smiled back at him.

'I can do this.'

'Okay, let's get moving,' said Joel as he stepped out towards the place to where Chris was pointing. 'Did it see you?'

'I don't know - it might have. It fell to the ground when I caught sight of it. Look! There it is again.'

'Keep still,' Joel ordered. 'Don't move a muscle.'

Joel strained his eyes against the darkness and about forty feet away he could see something lift its head above the bush it was hiding behind. Chris was right; it had horns – big black spiralling horns, on top of a bulbous black head. As it continued to rise out of the undergrowth, Joel could make out a large black - possibly hairy - body. Its shoulders were wide and falling from them were two incredibly muscular arms.

Joel recounted a book about mythical creatures he once read and this beast ahead of him, resembled one of those creatures, right up to the tip of its horns.

'It's a minotaur,' croaked Joel in disbelief.

'Don't be daft – they're only a myth,' said Chris hastily before squinting his own eyes and seeing the beast stand up tall for himself. He looked at Joel.

'You're right,' he gulped. 'It's a minotaur. What's a Minotaur doing here – this isn't Ancient Greece?'

'We're in a world with knights, dragons, goblins and fairies, Chris,' said Joel mockingly. 'Are you really that surprised?'

'Er...Joel,' said Caitlin sheepishly.

'Quiet, Caitlin – it might hear you.'

Suddenly, another creature appeared from the undergrowth to the left of the minotaur. It had two heads – one of a lion, the other of a goat. On its rear a tail rose above its back, and it made a soft hissing sound.

'A chimera,' Joel said quietly.

'There's something coming, Joel,' piped Caitlin, looking in the opposite direction to the boys.

'Look!' said Chris. 'There's more.'

He was right, behind the minotaur and chimera, a small host of ugly, fierce looking beasts rose up shyly from the ground, as if they had just come out from a long game of hide-and-seek wondering where the seeker had gotten to.

'Joel! It's getting closer,' said Caitlin, her voice rising in volume.

Joel turned around sharply. 'Caitlin, you need to keep qui...'

He didn't finish his sentence.

'Joel! They're coming.' Caitlin's voice turned to a shriek.

Something was bounding through the long grass right at them. They couldn't see what it was, but if they didn't move fast, it would be right at their ankles in seconds.

Joel threw his head around to see a small multitude of mythical creatures peering through the darkness at them, but they hadn't seemed to move. He had a make a split decision. They had to run, but in which direction.

He looked back at the rapidly approaching movement in the long grass and saw that whatever it was had grown in numbers. He decided to run towards what he could see rather than what he could not.

'RUN!' he shouted, and Caitlin and Chris followed him as they charged in the direction of the minotaur and chimera – all three of them screaming as they ran.

The beasts ahead of them also began to roar and bleat, and to the children's astonishment they also turned and began to run in the same direction as them, as if they too were running for their lives.

Chris glanced over his shoulder to see the grass still swishing and swashing as though it was being beaten by a strong wind. Whatever it was behind them, it was to be feared, especially if it made a minotaur run away from it.

Without warning the trees bean to separate and the horde of beasts all ran frenziedly down a hill into what seemed to be a canyon; a cacophony of grunts and roars echoing off the damp, stone walls. For a split-second Joel felt like a cowboy corralling his wild stallions until he remembered that he too was being corralled.

Caitlin's scream intensified which seemed to urge the creatures in front of her to increase their volume too.

And then, the beasts suddenly came to an abrupt halt as the two walls of the canyon became one and they came to a dead end; each creature jostling with its neighbour trying to hide behind one another, the roars and howls now changing to whimpers and sobs of despair. A small, rare shaft of sunlight lit up the blocked passageway, putting all the creatures in full view of Joel, Caitlin, and Chris, who also came to a sudden stop only feet away from the bared teeth of the chimera, only it didn't growl or snap at them. Instead, it appeared to withdraw its head away from them.

Caitlin, however, carried on screaming and this encouraged the army of animals to do the same.

Chris looked back again and the grass they had been running through had become shorter and whatever was chasing them was about to show itself – it was coming fast. It was now only twenty feet away.

Fifteen.

Ten.

Five.

The grass stopped swaying and suddenly it parted and out jumped about thirty extremely fluffy buck-toothed white rabbits, with enormous brown eyes. They landed only a yard or two in front of Joel - who had quickly put himself between his siblings and their pursuers - and they began to laugh hysterically as the lead rabbit appeared to point at them and said something to his fellow bunnies.

The children had seen nothing like it before and their screaming ceased immediately. The way the rabbits laughed was almost human. It was uncanny. They had been chased for nothing more than a cheap thrill by some long-haired, bug-eyed rodents.

The fixed look of fear that had covered the children's faces for the past two or three minutes fell and was replaced by stares of incredulity.

'Caitlin,' said Joel calmly. 'Do you think you could manage one more ear-piercing scream?'

'Certainly,' she replied, knowing exactly what Joel wanted.

She stepped in front of her brothers, bent down towards the rabbits, and screamed an almighty high-pitched scream.

Now it was the rabbits turn to be scared out of their wits. Their long ears stood straight up, their laughing ceased immediately, with one even dropping his fluffy little tail in fright, before turning on their short legs and hopping away faster than they had come.

'Stupid bunnies,' Caitlin muttered as she watched them bounce through the grass and out of sight into the darkness.

She turned around with a victorious smile, but that didn't last long either as she locked eyes with a minotaur who blew a hard breath from his large nostrils.

She screamed once more, and the once quiet monsters matched her tone.

Joel also squealed and was about to tell Caitlin and Chris to run, when one of the creatures - a vile looking troll - spoke through his whimpering.

'Please!' it pleaded. 'We don't want any trouble. Please don't hurt us.'

Joel stopped squealing and looked tentatively from creature to creature and realised that not one of them looked angry or menacing. In fact, every one of them looked nervous and scared.

'Are we in Narnia?' joked Chris uneasily. 'But without the Turkish delight.'

Joel slowly lifted his arms in an attempt to calm the beasts down. 'It's okay – we're not going to harm you. We're not here to cause any trouble.'

The fearful whimpering began to quieten down and some of the creatures began to straighten up out of their frightened poses.

'We're not your enemy,' said Joel. 'If anything, we thought you'd be harming us.'

The lion head on the chimera pulled out from behind the goat head and spoke.

'Why would we harm you – we don't know you?' it asked.

'Well...' Joel started anxiously. 'Because you're all vicious creatures; I mean, look at you. You're all minotaurs, trolls, two-headed dogs, and I've no idea what the rest of you are. You're all known for killing, destroying or being a nuisance.' His gaze fell on a group of sprites.

The minotaur took a sharp intake of breath, placing a massive hand on his chest, as if in shock.

'Killing and destroying?' it repeated. 'Why would you say such a thing? I've never harmed another living creature my entire existence.'

'My neither!' insisted a one-eyed giant.

'Nor me!' added a pointy-nosed sprite. 'I wouldn't dream of doing anything annoying.'

'But it's what you do,' said Joel. 'You're meant to do those things. You're supposed to be mean and aggressive.'

'Maybe where you come from,' bleated the goat-head, 'but in Dreadwood forest we live in harmony as one big happy family. We don't harm anyone, and we certainly don't kill.'

'Yeah,' interrupted a vampire-like animal. 'We're peaceful folk. And we get nervous when unknowns like you come onto our land.'

'Well, what about those horrid little bunny rabbits?' asked Chris.

'They're our friends. We were in the middle of a game of Marco Polo when you turned up!' said a woman with snakes for hair. 'Now they'll go and hide, and we won't be able to find them for days. It was you we were running from.'

'Oh,' said Chris. 'Our bad!'

Joel turned to the vampire-like creature.

'Unknowns? What do you mean? So, do other people do come into the forest?'

'Sometimes, but not very often,' said the minotaur. 'We see them, but we always hide, and we don't get seen. Do you know you're the first unknowns I've ever spoken to?' he smiled as he scratched his head. 'In fact, the more I think about it, apart from those two unknowns who passed through the other day, you're the only other people who have visited the forest for years and years. Don't know why, but we've come to like it this way – it's real homely like and peaceful.'

The beastly horde all nodded and smiled in agreement.

'No-one bothers us, and we have the whole forest to ourselves,' snorted a satyr. 'Well almost.'

'What do you mean, almost?' asked Caitlin who had gained confidence after realising that these creatures weren't going to harm her.

'Well apart from the old woman,' he replied.

'Who lives in a cottage in the middle of the forest?' asked Joel excitedly.

'Yes, that'll be her. She's always out and about in the forest collecting herbs and fruits and sap from the trees. She keeps us busy trying to hide from her. It's almost like a game now, but she hasn't spotted us yet.'

The children looked at each other hurriedly.

'Can you take us to her?' asked Chris.

'Why do you want to see her?' asked the minotaur.

'We need her help to rescue a princess for a friend of ours. If we don't rescue her, it's quite possible we won't be able to go home,' said Caitlin quietly. 'And I really want to go home.'

Joel knelt and looked at Caitlin.

'Why do you want to go home, Caitlin?' he asked. 'There's nothing there for us.'

Chris sidled over to them.

'It may not be great,' he said. 'But it's where we belong, Joel. Look around. This isn't our home. And I don't want to live a life where we're always running away from things and putting our lives in danger. I mean it's fun when I'm dreaming, but not when its reality. I just want to wake up and live a normal life.'

Caitlin nodded.

'Me too, 'she said.

Joel thought about what they had said. He looked around at all the talking creatures and then up into the dark tree canopy. He knew they were right, and he knew they had to take responsibility for themselves if their aunt and uncle weren't going to do it for them. He'd also started to lose sight of the reason they were in this mess in the first place. Dorian was counting on them.

He stood up and took Caitlin's right hand.

'Yeah, you're right. Our lives are what we make them. We've got to wake up at some point and face reality. But first, we've got a princess to rescue.'

He turned to the monstrous gathering behind him.

'Who can take us to the old woman?'

'I'm sorry,' said the satyr as he began to walk back out of the canyon. 'I promised the kids I teach them how to play the pipes today. Got to go. Nice to have met you though.'

Several other creatures also made their apologies and headed off, giving excuses as they went.

A tall cyclops came forward and said he'd be happy to take them to the old woman's cottage, but he insisted they told the old woman nothing about the creatures.

Joel promised him that they wouldn't say a word.

'It's a deal,' said the cyclops. 'But it's dinner time, and you ain't going anywhere till you've had a decent meal. Come with me, my missus does a mean nut roast. Mmm, tasty!'

Maynard Tait

CHAPTER 18

After eating a much-needed meal with some of the creatures, the Cyclops told the children to follow him, and as they walked back into the dense forest he asked if they knew any songs they could sing on their way, to make the journey more enjoyable. Chris happily obliged and started them off with his rendition of The Proclaimers 'I'm Gonna Be', to the apparent enjoyment of their guide who noisily stomped his way through the trees keeping very closely to the rhythm.

Joel guessed it had taken about two hours to reach the old woman's cottage, and by now any sign of the sun had completely disappeared and it was almost pitch black save for a small amount of candlelight coming from a window of the cottage.

The Cyclops left the children once he knew the cottage was close by, and he headed back towards his home singing

'Monster Mash' which Chris had taught him as they walked. After the first verse, however, he stopped. He turned around and frowned as he thought about what the children had said about him and all his friends, and he pondered their predicament. He fixed his eye on the children just as they disappeared out of sight then quickly turned back to his path and ran home as fast as he could.

***

The forest was still and eerily quiet now and as they hunched down in the grass, they discussed what the best way to approach the old woman would be.

'Dorian said she has ears like a hawk,' Chris reminded them. 'So, she'll probably hear us coming no matter how quiet we are.'

Just then, the candle went out. They heard a door close, and a cool breeze brushed past them.

'How right you are, sweetie,' said the old woman, whose warty visage appeared inches from their faces, eerily lit by candlelight.

All three screamed and jumped back a step, triggering a rope net that closed around them and hauled them up several feet off the ground.

'Hee, hee, hee,' the old woman cackled. 'Works every time.'

'Let us down,' Joel ordered with authority – the three children writhing around inside the net.

'All in good time, my little precious,' the old woman sneered. 'First I need to prepare my cauldron and then I'm going to stew you in it with dead troll and pieces of unicorn intestine and feed you to my pet alligators. I'm you're worst nightmare. Prepare to meet your doom!' She cackled menacingly until Chris interrupted her.

'No, you're not.'

'Eh?' said the old woman, surprised. 'Oh yes I am. My legend is famous in these 'ere parts – I'm the most powerful magician in the land.' She cackled some more.

'You're not a magician,' said Caitlin confidently. 'You're just a lonely old woman who can cast a handful of silly spells and make potions. And as far as you know nobody else lives in the forest, so you haven't killed any trolls or unicorns, because you don't even believe they exist, do you - and you certainly don't have any alligators.'

The old woman stared through the net at the three children.

'So, you're not frightened then?' she said meekly.

'Not in the least,' replied Joel.

She moved a little closer.

'Not even a little bit?'

'Not even,' Chris answered.

The old woman huffed and took out a knife from under her cloak.

'Oh, alright then. I was just having a bit of fun. Down you come,' she said as she reached as high as she could and cut a piece of rope. Suddenly, the children fell to the ground, and they grappled their way out of the net.

'You can come in for a nice hot cuppa and tell me what you're doing in the middle of Dreadwood Forest at this time of night. It's like Pickle Lilly circus round 'ere. I've never had so much pedestrian traffic,' said the old woman as she made her way back to the cottage.

The children brushed themselves down and followed the vanishing light of the candle the old woman was carrying.

'She's barmy,' said Chris.

'Well, you would be if you'd lived alone in this place for years,' said Joel. 'Now be nice. We need her help remember?'

Joel, Chris, and Caitlin entered the cottage and looked around at the bottles of potions, the skeleton in the corner, the cauldron that hovered over the fire, and a large book that lay open on a table in the centre of the room. The old woman busied herself at a stove, removing a tray of freshly baked biscuits from the oven.

''Ere you are. 'Ave one o' these,' she offered. 'You look like you 'aven't eaten anything in ages.'

'Oh, we're not long after a nut...' Chris started until Joel elbowed him in his side and gave him a hard stare.

'Sorry dear?' said the old woman.

'Oh, nothing,' said Chris.

The old woman set the tray on the table next to the book and the children took a biscuit each and began to munch on them.

'Mmm. Strawberry and chocolate?' asked Chris curiously.

'No,' Joel intervened. 'Raspberry and chocolate, I think.'

'Definitely, raspberry,' added Caitlin. 'But I'm not sure it's chocolate.'

The old woman began to pour the tea.

'Not even close. It's frogspawn and rabbit droppings.'

All three spat out the contents of their mouths and reached for a mug of tea to wash away any crumbs hanging around behind their teeth. The old woman looked slightly bemused.

'I've no idea what strawbrys or rasbrys are, but I've heard of this chocolate before. Never 'ad it mind – only for the rich is what oive 'eard. Now, drink yer tea and tell me what yer doin' 'ere. And yes, it is tea, just in case you were wonderin'.'

'We were sent to find you by Prince Dorian of Sallowell, to help make a potion that would waken his wife, Princess Freya, from her sleep. He said you made a potion for his brother Alfrek and that the only way to reverse it was by using Dream Weavers to create another one. Is that true?'

The old woman looked shocked as she fell back into a rocking chair next to the fire. She couldn't quite believe what she was hearing.

'You mean...it worked. He...He...travelled through time and space to another world. It really worked?'

'Yes,' said Chris. 'Your portion worked, but he ran out of it and has been living in our world for several years trying to find us.'

'Several years?' the old woman questioned. 'Why he only left here yesterday! And you're...you mean...you're the Dream Weavers?'

'Well, that's what he told us,' said Joel. 'And it may have only been a day for you, but he's been living in Kent for years.'

'Well, I never,' the old woman chuckled. 'I told him to come back before he ran out of potion. I warned him. And now he's stuck there. In Kent. What's Kent?'

'Don't worry about that. Can't you give us the recipe for the potion, so that when we return, we can make it there and then Dorian can drink it and come back here?' Caitlin asked.

'No, no. By the sounds of it, we don't have the same things in our worlds. No, he's definitely stuck there,' said the old woman rising to her feet, shaking her head. 'Such a shame. Quite a looker he was. But you're 'ere to waken the princess, and that I can help you wiv. Now, let's 'ave a look at this here recipe book and see if you three can do some magic.'

The old woman flicked through the pages to find the 'Reversals' section and proceeded to read out a list of ingredients, most of which the children had never heard of.

'Now, I'll 'ead out and round up these ingredients. I won't be long, but you three need to work out how we're goin' to get our 'ands on these last three things needed for the potion – coz without 'em, we ain't making anything. You're the Dream Weavers after all, so it's up to you.' The old woman grabbed an empty basket and left the cottage. 'Back in a jiffy,' she shouted as she pulled the door shut behind her.

'What does she mean?' asked Caitlin as the three gathered around the book and read through the recipe.

Joel put his finger to the recipe and ran it down the list of ingredients until he got to the bottom. It read;

A snip of boldness, a drop of fear,
The warmth of love you now mix here,
Weave your dreams and make them real,
Waken the sleeping, and they will heal.

'What is that supposed to mean?' asked Chris.

'I've no idea,' Joel said bluntly. 'They're not exactly things you can buy in a shop or pick from a bush. Oh, it's no use,' he added despairingly, sitting on the bench next to the table. 'We can't do this. We should've just stayed at home. What was Dorian thinking? That we would have what it takes to do this. We're just three kids with over-active imaginations. We can't do magic. Any powers we've had have all but disappeared.' He began to think about what Dorian had said at the dinner table. *'If you're not careful, you might not wake up at all and your dreams may just become your reality'.*

'For all we know this used to be our dreams – but now it's probably real. We may be stuck here forever.'

Chris and Caitlin sat down either side of Joel and Caitlin rested her cheek on her eldest brother's arm. She began to cry, and Joel put an arm around her to comfort her.

'I'm scared,' she cried.

'I know,' said Joel. 'But we're all together. That's all that matters. We'll find a way to get home. Trust me.'

'I wish our real mum and dad were here,' Chris added. 'I bet they'd know what to do.'

Joel threw his other arm around Chris and all three sat together, not knowing what to do.

Caitlin's eyes welled-up. A tear rolled down her cheek and fell into her mug of tea. It made a plopping sound as it hit the warm liquid, just as Joel blew at Chris's hair that was beginning to tickle his cheek.

Then without warning, Joel jumped to his feet.

'That's it,' he yelled.

'That's what?' asked the old woman as she came back into the cottage with her basket full of an array of what looked like mushrooms, berries, and weeds.

'The three ingredients. Quickly,' he said as he grabbed the basket from the old woman's hands and threw them all into an empty bowl he found lying on the floor. 'Get the water.'

The old woman grabbed a ladle and scooped some water out of the recently boiled kettle and poured it into the bowl and she began to mix it all around with a wooden spoon. She glanced at the recipe book and checked that she had collected everything.

'What is it, Joel?' Chris asked.

'It's so obvious – we've had the ingredients all the time,' he replied.

'It is? We have?'

'Yes! Old woman, have you got all the right ingredients?' asked Joel.

'Well, let me see,' she replied, looking into the bowl of mixture. 'So, that's one sprig of alfen, one handful of shooshrooms, two hand grabs of pilsplat berries, and three twigs from a belchden tree. Yes, yes, that's everything. All we need now are your three ingredients, my boy,' she grinned.

'Okay! Listen.' Joel picked up the potions book. 'Chris, what's the one quality you have buckets of when you're Sir Chris of Scamalot?'

'Err…bravery?' Chris replied.

'Or also known as…boldness,' said Joel.

'Well, I guess so – I've never thought about it much.'

'What we need to do is add some of your boldness into the mixture. Old woman, have you any scissors?'

'What are sizzers?' she answered, perplexed by the question.

'Er…cutting implements,' said Caitlin. 'Things that go snip, snip.'

'Oh,' laughed the old woman opening a drawer under the table, taking out what can only be described as scissors. 'I don't know about sizzers, but I've got these wanglers, will they do?'

'Absolutely,' said Joel taking the wanglers from the old woman. 'Chris, turn around.'

'Why?'

'I need to cut your hair.'

'What? No way.'

'Chris, *a snip of boldness*. You're bold, so a snip of your hair should so the trick.'

Chris pursed his lips then reluctantly agreed.

'Okay – but only a snip.'

Joel cut a small amount of hair from the crown of Chris's head and dropped it into the mixture.

'Now for '*a drop of fear*', said the old woman.

Joel turned to Caitlin and took her hands in his.

'Caitlin, I need you to think of the most fearful thing you can imagine. The one thing that scares you the most. Your tears are formed by fear, so we need one for the potion. Do you think you can do it?'

Caitlin dropped her head and gazed down at the table, nodding her head gently.

'Good girl,' said Joel as he ripped of a leaf from the belchden tree twig and held it up to Caitlin's right cheek.

It only took a few seconds for Caitlin's eyes to fill up and she gulped hard, followed by a sniff. Then the tears came, and Joel caught a couple on the leaf he was holding.

'I'm sorry, Caitlin,' said Joel. 'I hope it wasn't too painful.'

'What did you think about? What was the scariest thing you could imagine?' Chris asked inquisitively.

Joel shot an angry look at Chris.

'It doesn't matter,' he snorted angrily.

'Not remembering my real mum and dad and knowing I'll never see them again,' said Caitlin quietly.

Joel signed heavily and laid his empty hand on Caitlin's shoulder.

'You don't know that. They might turn up one day. We've got to believe that.'

Joel then dropped Caitlin's tears into the bowl and the old woman mixed it all around with the ladle. Nothing happened apart from a sweet-smelling aroma that rose from the mixture.

'Now for the '*warmth of love*',' said the old woman.

'Oh yeah,' said Chris sarcastically. 'That'll be easy. Let me just empty my pockets and dump some in.'

'It is easy,' Joel said firmly. 'We're a family. We may not say how we feel about each other much of the time, but...'

Chris scrunched up his face as if he'd had his tongue stung by a wasp.

'You mean never. We don't do that sort of thing.'

'But,' Joel continued. 'I think it's safe to say that we love each other, and if mum and dad were here, then we'd know that real love more than we could ever imagine or dream of. So, if we think about that for a moment, maybe that'll be enough for the potion to work.'

Chris looked at Joel as if he'd just fallen into a vat of love potion.

'I suppose you want us to hug again too,' he joked.

'That's a good idea,' said Caitlin.

'I was kidding,' said Chris.

'Well, it wouldn't hurt,' said Joel raising both of his arms. 'Let's do it.'

Caitlin shuffled into Joel's side and wrapped her arms around his waist, but Chris stood his ground.

'I ain't hugging,' he muttered.

'Chris, this could be our only chance. It takes a bold person to do things that our outside of his comfort zone. Maybe you're not as bold as I thought.'

'Am too,' Chris responded.

'Then prove it, big mouth,' said the old woman. 'And stop dawdling!'

Chris shuffled uncomfortably.

'Okay, okay. I'll do it.'

'Yay! Family hug,' said Caitlin.

Chris sidled up against his brother and Joel closed his arm around him. He told them to close their eyes and to think of how it would be if their mum and dad were with them and of the happy times they would have together.

The old woman watched them closely as she continued to mix the ingredients together. A minute or two passed but nothing happened.

Chris opened one eye and looked down at the bowl and then at Caitlin and Joel.

'Well, this is awkward?'

'Shut up, Chris,' said Joel sternly.

Chris shut his eye again and they stood for another few seconds before opening his other eye.

'Maybe we should blow on it or something.'

'Of course,' said Joel as he opened his eyes. 'The warmth of love. You might be right, Chris.'

'I might?'

'It says '*The warmth of love mix here*'. If we breathe on it as we're thinking, perhaps that'll do it. Come on, lean in.'

The three children leant forward over the bowl.

'Now close your eyes and imagine mum and dad, then blow.'

All three closed their eyes, pouted their lips, and then began to blow gently into the mixture.

The old woman stared into the bowl and her eyes began to swell as the pleasant-smelling mixture started to bubble. Its colour began to change from green to red to brown then orange.

'It's working!' she gasped. 'It's actually working.'

The children opened their eyes and were amazed at the sight that unfolded before them. The potion swirled around the bowl as the solid twigs and berries dissolved into liquid. The sweet aroma filled their nostrils, and they began to laugh as a bright luminescence shone from the bowl lighting up the whole cottage.

Then very abruptly it stopped.

The swirling ceased, the liquid turned a greyish green colour and the shining light diminished.

'What's wrong?' asked Caitlin. 'Why did it stop?'

'I don't know,' said Joel.

'It's because you 'aven't finished the recipe,' said the old woman, lifting the book of potions into her hands. 'Weave your dreams and make them real' it says 'ere.

'Of course,' said Joel happily as he clutched at the necklace Dorian gave him. 'We've almost convinced ourselves that this is all real, but it isn't. It's still only a dream.'

'So, what do we do?' Chris asked.

'We have to remember what we can do in our dreams – no, more than that – who we are in them. Then remember how we got here in the first place, all together.'

Joel began to become very animated. 'Chris, remember Scamalot and bold Sir Chris, Princess Patience, and Twurp. Caitlin, think of how you feel when you are Caitlin the Fairy, guardian of the royal crown – tall, brave and fearless.'

'And you, Joel,' continued Chris. 'Are Agent Swift, protector of good, and... and...' He fumbled for words. 'Baker of the best banana muffins in the land.'

Caitlin and Joel glared at him.

'Sorry, it was all I could think of – but it's true!'

'Okay, let's try this one last time,' said Joel.

All three bent down over the potion.

'We are the Dream Weavers,' they said in unison.

Gently they began to blow on the liquid and immediately it started to bubble. It swirled around the bowl, and it glowed brightly, filling the whole cottage with an intense white light. A whirlwind rose from the bowl and everything else within the cottage got whirled around the place, except for the children who stood as still as rock, and the old woman who managed to grab hold of a table leg just in time.

The storm subsided after only a few seconds and the potion rested still in the bowl having turned an effervescent blue.

Joel smiled as he noticed his clothes. He was wearing his

black biker leathers and his hair was stylishly coiffured. He was Agent Swift once again.

Chris was dressed top to toe in light-weight armour, a golden sword strapped to his side.

Caitlin, however, was the only one not happy, but only because she had the back of her neck pressed hard against the roof of the cottage and the tips of her fairy wings were stuck in the rafters.

'Being an eight-foot fairy does have its downfalls, you know,' she said.

Joel and Chris laughed at the sight of her as she carefully folded her wings so not to damage them.

The bedraggled old woman staggered to her feet from the cold, damp floor and groaned as she peered into the pot at the reversing potion.

'Well, I'll just bottle this up and then put the kettle on again. I don't know about you lot, but I need another cup o' tea!'

PART FOUR

Maynard Tait

CHAPTER 19

The overwhelming darkness of the forest still shrouded everything, but its gloominess couldn't darken their spirits as the next part of their adventure began.

Joel, Chris, and Caitlin stood in front of the old woman's cottage determined to see this through to the end however it turned out.

The old woman shuffled up to them and wished them well on their quest.

'And if you see that ugly brute, Alfrek – you give him a piece of my mind. 'Ere,' she said to Joel, planting two small vials of liquid in his right hand.

'What are these?' he asked.

'That one's the reversing potion,' she said tapping one of the vials. Just put a drop into the mouth of the princess and she'll wake up immediately feeling healthier and stronger than ever. In fact, she'll never be ill again for the rest of her days nor anyone she loves. But it has to be one of you three that gives it to her remember, otherwise it won't work.'

'And the other one?' Joel asked.

'Well, that's something that might come in 'andy,' she replied. 'You'll know what to do when the time comes. Let's just say it'll make all your troubles disappear. But there's only enough for one dose so use it wisely. Now, off with ya. Go and be brave.'

'We will,' said Caitlin. 'And thank you – for everything.'

'You're welcome, my dear. Now go, go!' she shouted, shooing the children away. 'Evil waits for no man – or fairy.'

The three turned and headed away south towards Sallowell, their enemies and uncertainty before them, as a faint glimmer of sunlight pierced its way through the forest above them.

***

The sun was high in the sky by the time they reached the edge of the forest. The dense, depressing darkness gave way to soft, rolling hills to the south as far as the eye could see. They looked to the east and west and although they couldn't see the ends of the forest, they knew they were there, as were their hunters and hopefully, Pinky. Caitlin had hoped that they went in opposite directions. She couldn't help but think about what their enemies would have done to Marshmallow Man had they caught him.

'I just hope we made it out before they got around,' said Joel. 'Otherwise, they're ahead of us and we'll have the disadvantage. They'll find the princess and sit in wait for us to arrive.'

'Then we've no time to lose,' said Chris exuberantly. 'Sallowell is directly in front of us somewhere over these hills, so let's get moving.'

The three set off at a good pace, although for every three strides the boys took, Caitlin only took one. Her height was useful for seeing over rock formations and over smaller drumlins, as she looked for the most direct route forward.

They walked for what seemed like hours when suddenly, Caitlin beckoned the boys to stop.

'We can't, Caitlin. We have to keep going,' said Joel.

'But I think I can hear something – just stop,' she snapped sharply, as she tossed her head around and stood motionless.

The boys came to a halt and copied their sister.

And there it was. It was the distant sound of an engine, perhaps two.

Caitlin bounded up the side of a small drumlin and immediately saw two quad bikes coming straight towards her some five hundred metres away, flanking the Black Night on his galloping charger.

'It's two of Pratt's men and the Black Knight,' she shouted to the others.

'That's okay,' said Chris boldly. 'We can take three of them.'

'Er…they're not alone,' Caitlin added.

The boys ran up to join her and they were stunned as they watched about forty quad bikes and a similar number of horses and knights come over the top of a hill closely following the Black Knight. The sound of the engines was almost deafening as it got closer and closer. Behind the riders a small army of goblins were in hot pursuit on large rodent like creatures.

'We need to get out of here!' bellowed Joel.

'We can't outrun them,' retorted Chris as he looked up at Caitlin. 'Well, she could, but what about us?'

Joel stared back at Chris incredulously.

'Of course, we can,' he exclaimed. 'We're still forgetting we're in our dreams. Look at us. We're Dream Weavers, so we can do whatever we normally do in our dreams. Come on, think of Bucktooth.'

Chris closed his both is eyes tight then quickly threw one open to find his trusty horse kneeling in front of him ready to be mounted.

'Bucktooth!' Chris cried. 'I knew I could trust in you.'

'Quick, Joel,' interrupted Caitlin. 'They're nearly on us. We need to leave.'

Joel smiled as he imagined his Kawasaki KX 450F dirt bike in front of him and within a blink of an eye there it was. He leapt onto it and started the engine.

'Try and keep up,' he yelled at Caitlin then suddenly his head was encased by his helmet. He twisted his throttle and pulled away quickly with Bucktooth close behind him.

'Oh, don't worry about me,' said Caitlin to herself, as she unfurled her wings. 'Why run when you can fly.'

She flapped her wings and took off after her brothers, their pursuers only a stone's throw away.

The terrain began to change after a short distance and small clumps of trees sprouted up causing Chris and Joel to swerve sharply at times to avoid colliding with them. It also made them slow down a little and the enemy was able to gain on them.

Caitlin took advantage of being able to fly. Looking down into the trees she spotted something glinting in the sunlight. As she hovered high above Joel and Chris, she could see Sallowell only a short distance ahead of them over the rolling hills. She looked and back and saw Pratt's henchmen fast approaching. She swooped down between the boys and told them to keep going as fast as they could.

'I can't stop the quad bikes, but I can distract the knights on horseback,' she called to Joel.

'Be careful!' he shouted back.

'I will,' she said before doing a loop in the air and doubling back on herself. She flew toward a clump of trees and landed in a large jay's nest that was full of silver jewellery and goblets studded with precious gems. Gathering as much of the contents of the nest as she could carry, she plummeted toward the oncoming goblins who were by now out in front of the knights.

The sunshine caught the colours of the gems, and the all the goblins suddenly turned their focus on the shiny treasure.

Caitlin turned left and then darted right across the front of the goblins. They yanked the reins on their ugly mounts and followed Caitlin's path causing them to crash into the horses and bring down most of the knights with a tremendous thud. Caitlin began to throw down some of the jewellery making some of the goblins forget who they were chasing, and they galloped after the falling diamonds and gold instead, getting in the way of all the other knights who were thrown from their rides - including the Black Knight, but not before he had removed a net from his back and thrown it high up into the air as hard as he could.

Caitlin saw it coming just too late and the net wrapped around her closing her wings and bringing her down to the ground.

Joel glanced over his shoulder to see Caitlin land on a haystack. He pulled hard on his brakes and his bike skid to a halt, Chris pulling Bucktooth up beside it.

Caitlin shouted at them to get to Sallowell.

Joel looked toward Sallowell and then back at Caitlin, with Pratt and his henchmen between them gaining ground with every second.

'Joel,' shouted Chris.

Joel looked again toward Sallowell thinking about Princess Freya and Dorian.

'Joel, Caitlin needs us!'

If they got caught then they'd be trapped in this dream world forever, he had to rescue the princess.

'Joel! What are you waiting for? She needs us,' yelled Chris.

He looked back at Caitlin who was now surrounded by some of the goblins and two of the fallen knights. What should he do? Follow his dreams or save his family?

His eyes caught Caitlin's and he remembered the promise he had made to Caitlin that last morning when they were late to school – *I promise I won't leave you behind ever again.*

Joel revved his engine and spun his bike around to face the oncoming enemy.

'How are we going to do this?' shouted Chris who had turned Bucktooth around to mirror Joel.

'Time for a bit of jousting, don't you think, Sir Chris?' answered Joel.

Chris smiled back.

'Yeah! Good idea.'

Chris raised his right arm to a ninety-degree angle and immediately a ten-foot-long lance appeared locked in place aimed directly at the nearest henchman. Its pole was made of burnished bronze, but its heavy weight was unrecognisable to its holder whose boldness and bravery filled him up with four times his normal strength. On the end of the pole was a boxing glove ready to make contact with the first receiver. He reared Bucktooth up on his hind legs then charged him forward. In seconds Chris had taken out three henchmen and their mechanical steeds.

Joel kicked his bike into gear and sped toward Caitlin who was struggling under the weight of the net. Some goblins had taken their booty and ridden away but those who weren't quick enough to get any jewels encircled Caitlin and were beginning to taunt her. It was the first time they had ever captured the Fairy Enforcer and they knew they'd get a huge reward from the Goblin King if they brought her in.

Joel evaded Pratt's henchmen as he got closer to Caitlin, but he didn't notice Pratt himself as he wove his way across the battlefield. Pratt reached down to his side and raised a crossbow and fired it. The arrow was perfectly placed and went through the spokes of Joel's front wheel. The motorcycle flipped forward and threw Joel high into the air, and he landed on the haystack next to Caitlin.

Chris saw what had happened and he too became distracted. He steered Bucktooth toward Joel and Caitlin and rode hard, but he didn't notice the Black Knight mount a horse and gallop toward him with his own lance instantaneously appearing in his grasp. Chris caught the end of the black lance full in his side and the force of it sent him tumbling off the back of Bucktooth landing on his backside next to the haystack as Joel rolled out of it next to him and Caitlin. A goblin ran up and threw a net over all of them to stop them from escaping.

Professor Pratt and the Black Knight stood side by side towering over their young enemies with the snivelling goblin in between.

Joel and Chris sat dazed and confused from their bruising dismounts.

'Told you I'd get you in the end didn't I, Swift,' cackled Pratt as he raised a pistol toward Joel. 'You made a fool of me too many times, and now it's over. I win.'

'And I vowed I'd take my revenge, Sir Chris,' roared the Black Knight as he lifted a sword high above his head ready to strike. 'Prepare for the afterlife!'

Joel, Chris, and Caitlin were cornered.

There was no escape.

They sat motionless, anticipating what was about to come, and then Chris muttered.

'No thanks,' he said.

The Black Knight cocked his head to the side.

'Excuse me?' he asked. 'What do you mean 'no thanks?''

'I mean I don't want to prepare for the afterlife. I'm not quite ready to go yet if it's alright with you.'

'But it's a phrase,' said the Black Knight slightly exasperated. 'And no, it's not alright. I'm not actually allowing you real time to prepare yourself, it's what one says when one's about to take someone's life.'

'And I think you'll find that I've won,' said Joel to Professor Pratt.

'No, Swift. I'm the one with the gun pointing at you. I can't see how you think that puts you in a winning position. Now, if you don't mind, we've got a job to do.'

Suddenly, as Pratt began to squeeze on his trigger and the Black Knight tightened his grip on his hilt, the sun disappeared from their view, and they were covered in shadow.

The goblin stopped his snivelling and all three turned quickly to see an enormous, gooey, pink foot coming down on top of them.

There was only a moment to scream before they were engulfed in marshmallow and encased in Marshmallow Man's foot.

'Oh Pinky!' cried Caitlin.

'Good use of distraction technique, Chris,' laughed Joel.

'Thanks. I'm just glad Pinky's so soft he didn't make any noise running over those hills otherwise he would have given the game away,' said Chris. 'You made it in the nick of time though, big fella!'

Marshmallow Man reached down and lifted the nets from the three, gave a thumbs up and then proceeded to shake his foot to try and release the other three entombed in it, but to no avail, so he gave up. Instead, he turned and ran after any loose goblins and wandering knights, chasing them back to wherever they came from.

'Go get 'em, Pinky!' Caitlin cheered.

Joel, Chris, and Caitlin got to their feet and dusted themselves off. Caitlin fluttered her wings to check they were still working.

'Wow!' said Joel. 'Things certainly are becoming more and more real by the minute. That was all too close for comfort, but at least we don't have any arch-rivals to worry about anymore. All we need to do now is get to Prince Heldrek's castle and waken up Princess Freya, and then hopefully we'll wake up back home and we can tell Dorian she's safe.'

'All sounds too easy,' said Chris.

'Yeah, I know, but we'd better get a move on. I feel the longer we stay here the more likely we'll remain here.'

'Well, Sallowell's just over that hill,' said Caitlin pointing to the south as she rose into the sky. 'I can see it from here. It shouldn't take long to get there. Not if you use your transport like before.'

Joel looked at his dirt bike lying next to the haystack. It was completely ruined. He wouldn't be riding that again. At least not in this dream.

Chris watched in dismay as Bucktooth rode off further and further into the distance.

'Yeah, I think we need something else to finish this journey,' he uttered.

'I have just the thing,' smiled Joel.

As soon as he had spoken jet packs appeared on his and Chris's backs.

'Cool!' exclaimed Chris. 'This is awesome.'

'Just pull the lever in your right hand to go up and slowly release it to come down. Lean to whichever way you want to go,' Joel instructed.

'Sure thing, sounds simple,' said Chris as he shot up into the sky.

Caitlin had to swoop to her left to avoid being hit. He banked left, then right, then right again, screaming joyfully all the while. 'This is so awesome!'

'Take it easy, you twonk!' shouted Joel as he jetted upwards after his young brother.

Maynard Tait

CHAPTER 20

Back in Kent, Dorian paced the bedroom floor becoming more and more worried by the minute. Joel, Caitlin, and Chris had been sleeping for twenty hours now and there was no sign of them about to waken.

'Oh, what was I thinking?' Dorian shouted, slapping his forehead with the palm of his head. 'I knew it would be too dangerous. I was being selfish. I shouldn't have made them go. What can I do?'

He rubbed his head in a vain attempt to ease a headache he had had for the past couple of hours. Dorian had not slept himself overnight, choosing instead to remain in the room with the children hoping they'd only be a few minutes or an hour at the most.

He went to the kitchen to look for something to take to help the headache. He opened several cupboards but there was nothing useful.

'Water. Cold water,' he uttered.

He opened the fridge to get the cold jug of water, but it was practically empty.

'Aw, come on,' he said exasperated. 'Who does that?'

He was about to close the fridge door when he spotted a bottle carefully placed behind some mouldy cheeses. He took out the bottle and read the label. It said in bold, red letters.

SWIFTS SECRET SMOOTHIE
DO NOT DRINK
DANGEROUS TO NON-DREAMERS
YOU HAVE BEEN WARNED

Dorian chuckled.

'Kids!' he said.

He pulled out the stop and tentatively sniffed at the greyish liquid inside.

'Hmm, fruity. Notes of dark berries with an undertone of smoked barrels. Not completely unpleasant.'

Although he knew there was nobody else in the house, except for the kids who were fast asleep upstairs, he glanced around him to check no-one was watching then took a quick swig of the smoothie directly from the bottle.

He swished it around his mouth and swallowed just before he began to wretch and gag.

'Ugh! That is revolting.' He banged the stop into the bottle and placed it back in the fridge exactly where he found it then slammed it shut.

'Dangerous?' he said to himself. 'Should be illegal!'

***

It took them about half an hour to reach the castle. They landed in the middle of the courtyard, and it was clearly market day, as many stalls laden with various types of goods covered the cobbles and there were many people out shopping. The locals had never seen people flying before or an eight-foot-tall fairy, and it took Joel quite a while to convince them that they weren't sorcerers or wizards, but the people did seem genuinely pleased to meet them, especially when they said they were friends of Dorian. Some even bowed thinking they must have been very important people if they knew the prince, or even royalty.

They asked the nearest vendor where they could find Prince Heldrek. He pointed across the courtyard to two enormous doors.

'He'll be in the great hall, sitting by his daughter's side, no doubt,' said the vendor.

'Princess Freya's here?' asked Joel.

'Yes. Prince Heldrek brought her back from the garden cottage so he could protect her from that brute son of his, Alfrek. Nobody knows where he is anymore. Prince Dorian thinks he's hiding in the forbidden forest and went looking for him a couple of days ago. But I reckon he's a bit closer than that, waiting for the right moment to strike and snatch the princess away.'

'Come on,' said Joel to the others. 'He could be right. Alfrek could be lurking anywhere around here. The quicker we get in there the quicker we can give Freya the potion and she'll wake up, stronger and healthier for ever.'

They turned on their heels and ran through the market.

The vendor who was talking with them noticed a hairy hand reach out from under a cloak of a tall figure standing at the end of his stall, taking hold of an apple.

'Oi! You there. No thieving or I'll call the castle guards,' he shouted, as he turned to serve another customer.

The hand released the fruit, but it began to rot the moment it was let go.

The figure turned and lifted its head to reveal deep, dark, devilish eyes set deep into its ugly, repulsive face.

'Stronger and healthier forever,' Alfrek muttered. 'Suddenly I'm feeling very thirsty.'

Two tall guards blocking the doors of the great hall stepped forward and levelled their spears at the fast-approaching children.

'Halt!' shouted one. 'State your business!' said the other.

'We need to see Prince Heldrek,' answered Chris. 'We've been sent by Prince Dorian to save Princess Freya.'

'Oh yeah?' asked the taller one of the guards. 'Prove it.'

All three grabbed at their necklaces and held them out for the guards to see.

'These are part of the royal medallion Dorian received from his parents on his thirteenth birthday,' said Joel hurriedly. 'He gave us a piece each to help guide us here. He has the fourth part. Prince Heldrek will recognise it straight away.'

The two guards considered the necklaces for a moment then looked at one another and nodded.

'Alright, fair enough,' said the shorter one as he twisted a large handle and pushed the door open. 'You can go in.'

Joel and Caitlin moved forward thanking the guards and stepped into the cavernous hall, but Chris was stopped by the taller guard.

'Only two visitors at a time, mate. Don't want to crowd the patient.'

'What?' said Chris. 'This isn't a hospital, you know!'

'Them's the rules,' ordered the shorter one.

Chris looked at Joel.

'Look it's fine, Chris. It only needs to be one of us anyway,' said Joel. 'You stay outside and help keep an eye out for Alfrek and we'll see to the princess.'

'Okay,' Chris responded reluctantly.

The door closed behind the two and Chris loitered next to the guards.

The shorter guard looked up and down at Chris.

'Nice armour,' he offered.

'Thanks,' Chris replied. 'It's...er...adamantium.' Then he quickly crossed his forearms and scowled at them like a mutant super-hero.

The two guards shuddered. Chris laughed.

'Go on, clear off,' snapped the taller guard. 'Go and wait for your mates somewhere else. We're on duty here, not you!'

Chris moved away and wandered around the market, keeping his eyes peeled for any strange looking people. He didn't know what Alfrek looked like, but he got the impression from the old woman that they'd certainly know him if they saw him. He noticed a small crowd on the opposite side of the pond laughing and cheering, so he made his way over. He glanced up at the statues poised in the centre of the pond and smiled at the way the two figures were entwined, the muscular male figure's arms wrapped protectively around the female, their hands clasped tightly together, their faces blank of any features.

His attention was grabbed by a shout from the middle of the small crowd.

'Hey, you! Brave knight.'

Chris looked to see the gathering open and a middle-aged man beckoning him to join them.

'Come, sir, would you like to see some magic. I guarantee this is magic like you have never seen before.'

'I wouldn't bet on it,' muttered Chris as he walked toward the crowd.

***

Joel and Caitlin walked quickly across the vast hall toward a bed at the opposite end. The space was modestly adorned with a few statues of Heldrek's ancestors and portraits of current family members. Benches and long tables lined the sides of the hall leaving the vast floor space empty except for the bed and several chairs placed around it. Enormous stained-glass windows let muted light in at both ends. One window depicted Dorian and Alfrek as victorious warriors, each with a raised foot resting on a conquered beast. The other window above the entrance doors showed a large red dragon looking down on the wide-open floor.

A man sat on a chair next to the bed, his head in his hands. Prince Heldrek.

Princess Freya lay on the bed her hands clasped together, the rise and fall of her chest the only evidence to proof that she wasn't actually dead.

It was silent.

It was dark.

And it was eerie.

Joel and Caitlin approached the silhouette of the prince.

'Your majesty,' said Joel.

Prince Heldrek spoke quietly and calmly through his hands and remained motionless.

'Whatever you think you have to offer, let it be known that all the wisest counsel has been sought over the past day and not one has been able to offer words of comfort or a remedy for my daughter-in-law's sorry state. The king and queen of Sallowell hold me and my family fully responsible for this foul deed and I remain at her side in the hope that one day, a comforter will come to correct all this wrong; my much-beloved son, Dorian, will return and his bride shall awaken. Until that day this stool shall be my resting place.'

'But your majesty, I have the cure,' said Joel. 'Your son, Dorian sent us here and I have a way to waken the princess. Look!'

Heldrek slowly lifted his head to see Joel holding a vial of potion in his hand. He stood to his feet as he gazed at the tiny bottle before looking up at Joel and then Caitlin.

'How do I know you speak the truth? How do you know my son?'

Joel put the vial back into his pocket and then he and Caitlin took out their medallion pieces to show Heldrek.

He stood, walked toward them, and clasped his large hands on Joel's shoulders.

'You do know him.'

'Yes, and he wanted you to know that he's safe and well after all these years.'

'Years?' questioned Heldrek. 'He only left here yesterday!'

'Er...yes,' fumbled Caitlin. 'But time sure can drag when you're away from home.'

Heldrek nodded.

'Yes, that is right, I am sure.' He then remembered the cure. 'But the potion, you say you have a potion?'

'Yes, I have it right here,' said Joel reaching into his pocket again.

He froze to the spot as soon as he felt something sharp poke into his back.

Caitlin turned to see a hideous creature reveal itself from under a long black cloak. Its eyes were large, deep, and dark like coal. Its hand holding the sword against her brother's spine was hairy and covered in warts. It stood as tall as she did but there was nothing she could do to help. The tip of the sword was needle thin and ready to pierce whatever was in its way.

***

Chris laughed heartily at the awful card tricks that the street magician did to woo the crowds.

'Call that magic? I'll show you some real magic,' he said.

'Okay then,' said the magician, removing his top hat from his head. 'How about this? With this knife, I'll take my hat and stab it. And with the whisk of its blade, I'll take from my hat…a rabbit'.

The magician pulled a baby rabbit from his hat and the crowd took a step back in amazement.

'Don't be daft. He's got a trap door in his hat. Look!' said Chris, as he snatched the hat from the magician and showed the crowd where he had hidden the fluffy animal. 'This is how you wow a crowd.'

Instantaneously Chris spun around, and his suit of armour turned into black tie and tails and cloak. The crowd all gasped. Chris removed his cloak.

'If you think a taking a rabbit out of a hat's impressive then watch this.'

He began to spin his cloak around with one hand while

waving the other. The crowd began to take a step back and then another as the cloak span and span.

'Don't be alarmed. I've never harmed anyone with a cloak yet,' Chris shouted.

The eyes of the crowd began to widen, and Chris could see they were impressed.

Continuing to spin the cloak he began his magic spell.

'To make something appear you just have to imagine...'

The crowd moved further and further away, their mouths gaping.

'...and out of your mind will appear a red...'

'Dragon!' wailed one of the crowd.

'No,' said Chris. 'a red...'

'DRAGON!' roared another as the crowd turned.

'No!' Chris repeated, dropping the cloak. 'a red rooster. Sorry, I'm not very good at rhyming.'

The crowd ran away, and stalls were overturned. Everyone screamed as they bumped into one another, and Chris was suddenly left standing on his own next to a clucking chicken.

'Wow! Tough crowd.'

The rooster ran after the crowd and Chris spun on his heels to see the reason for the rampage. It was Davina, Chris's two-headed pet dragon, gliding down over the castle - and she looked angry.

'Uh-oh!' whimpered Chris. 'Still cross about the itching powder, I see.'

She came lower and lower, and Chris quickly sprinted away as fast as his legs could carry him.

***

Prince Heldrek stared at the monster in front of him and saw the medallion burnt deep into his chest.

'Alfrek? Is that you?' he questioned.

'Yes, it's me, you fool, and I've come to take what is rightfully mine. I should have married Freya, not Dorian. And this is what I get for my trouble. To look like this.'

Alfrek threw off the cloak to reveal his disfigured body.

'But Alfrek, we'll get you help,' said Heldrek desperately.

'You can't help me,' he roared. 'But he can.'

Alfrek prodded the end of his sword against Joel's neck.

'The potion. Give me the potion.'

'I don't have any potion,' Joel chanced.

'Don't fool with me, boy,' Alfrek bellowed.

He reached into Joel's pocket and took out the vial and looked at it.

'Stronger and healthier forever is what you said. I'll drink this potion and I'll have power forever.'

'But what about Freya?' asked Caitlin.

'I'll take her to the forest and the old woman will make up another reversing potion for her, and we'll live together forever.'

'It won't work,' said Joel.

'We'll see about that,' replied Alfrek.

***

Chris ran in circles around the pond as Davina swooped down trying to catch him.

'Come on, Chris. Think', he shouted at himself as he ran toward the great hall. He went through his tricks in his mind that could bring down the great red dragon. As he reached the doors of the hall he stopped immediately.

'Got it. Shrinking bomb.'

Chris blinked his eyes and opened them to find a crossbow and a grenade in his hands. He aimed high above Davina who was banking around to dive down on top of her quarry. He pulled the trigger, and the arrow carried the grenade up over the dragon's head.

Alfrek stepped away from Joel his sword still raised.

He removed the stop from the vial and lifted it to his mouth.

The bomb exploded directly above Davina as she began her rapid descent. Glittery powder floated down on top of the dragon's wings and instantly they began to shrink. This confused her and sent her of course right into the stain-glass window above the great hall's doors, unable to hold her weight up in the air any longer.

The window shattered, and Chris dove to his left, crouching under one of the market stalls, just in the nick of time.

Alfrek turned at the sound of the crashing to see the stained-glass window shatter and Davina careering toward him. He quickly raised the vial to his mouth, but the dragon's long snout crash-landed at his feet and the collision threw him and the vial upwards, Joel and Caitlin diving to opposite sides of the giant creature.

Davina came to a stop, raised her right head with mouth agape, and Alfrek and the open vial fell into her fiery throat. She swallowed her meal and then, as if by magic, she vanished.

Chris burst through the doors just in time to catch his last ever glimpse of his pet dragon.

'Note to self,' he said. 'Itching powder is *so* not cool.'

Prince Heldrek fell to his knees.

'Nooo! My son,' he cried. 'And now Freya will sleep forever.'

Caitlin knelt by him and put her arm around him. 'I'm so sorry,' she said. 'I wish there were something we could do.'

'There is,' said Joel cheerfully.

'What do you mean?' asked Caitlin. 'The potion's gone and it didn't even do what the old woman said it would.'

'Not that potion anyway,' Joel smiled as he pulled another vial from a pocket. 'This is the potion for the princess. Alfrek didn't know I had two vials. Thankfully, he took the one the old woman wanted us to use in an emergency. And it worked. Remember what she said? *"it'll make all your troubles disappear"*. Well, it did that alright.'

'But where did they go?' asked Chris as he joined them by the bed. 'Davina and Alfrek?'

'Who knows,' Joel replied. 'But at least we know wherever it is, they got a one-way trip.'

Heldrek got to his feet and asked Joel for the vial of potion to give to the princess.

'I'm sorry, your highness, but it has to be one of us that gives it to her. That was the instruction.'

Joel opened the vial and gently rested it against the princess's mouth and tipped the sole drop of liquid into it.

A few seconds passed and then Princess Freya's eyelids fluttered. She unclasped her hands and took a deep breath. A smile came over her lips as she slowly opened her eyes.

'Good morning, my husband,' she said as her eyes adjusted to the dim light looking toward a figure at the foot of her bed.

'Good morning, my wife,' the figure replied.

Everyone turned to see who she was talking to.

'Dorian!' Chris exclaimed in surprise.

Dorian stood in his royal robes as he had done when he left Sallowell, and he hadn't aged a day.

'But how?' Joel asked. 'How did you get back?'

'Get back from where, my love,' asked Freya, who was now sitting up. 'And why am I not in the cottage? And father-in-law, what are you doing here with these strange looking infants?'

Dorian stepped forward and took Freya's hands, kissing them both.

'I'll explain later, my love. But go now with my father to the kitchens. You must be hungry after your long sleep. How about you prepare us some breakfast.'

'Anything special?' she asked sweetly.

He looked at the children.

'Pancakes,' replied Dorian. 'Lots of pancakes.'

Prince Heldrek helped Freya from her bed and led her away to the kitchens.

'Well?' Joel asked Dorian excitedly. 'How did you do it? We didn't think we'd see you until we got back home.'

Dorian put his arms around the children and drew them in to him.

'Well, you know that secret smoothie of yours at the back of the fridge?'

'Yeah,' said Chris crossly. 'The one that says DO NOT DRINK on it!'

'Well, let's just say I had a little sip and the next thing I knew I was sitting over a bowl of vomit in the old woman's cottage in Dreadwood Forest. If you don't mind me saying, you need to add a little sugar to take the edge off!'

Chris looked puzzled.

'You mean...drinking our smoothie is what got you back here?' he asked.

'Why, yes!' replied Dorian.

'I don't believe it,' said Joel. 'The smoothie is what helps us dream so much – it must be what makes us Dream Weavers.'

'And it was left to us by mum and dad,' added Caitlin.

'Maybe they left the recipe to you because they knew about your abilities,' said Dorian.

'But they would only have thought that if they knew about dream weaving,' said Joel 'or...'

He stopped talking.

'Or what?' asked Chris, frowning.

'Or they are Dream Weavers too,' Caitlin answered.

'Yes, Caitlin,' Joel added. 'If they were Dream Weavers too.'

Just then Chris slowly turned and started to walk out of the great hall.

'Chris?' called Dorian. 'Where are you going?'

'I wonder,' Chris said as he kept walking, so the others followed him outside.

CHAPTER 21

The sun was shining, and the market vendors and shoppers had returned to the courtyard to clear up the mess Davina had left behind.

Chris walked over to the pond that was in the centre of the courtyard. He looked up at the two figures that took centre stage, and a funny feeling came over him. There was something about them that looked familiar. He noticed it earlier, but he couldn't figure out what it was.

'Dorian?' he asked. 'How long have these statues been here?'

They all stopped and looked up at them.

'Oh, a few hundred years. The tale is told that they are two wizards who used their powers to make food and drink for the poor. The king at the time was selfish and proud and didn't treat the people at all well. He was worried that the people would revolt against him, so he had the last known royal sorcerer curse them to stone before they could flee. The king then banished the sorcerer to Dreadwood Forest and used an ancient spell, only the reigning king could use, to stop her from leaving it. Since then, people have been fearful of the forest and the magic it may contain. The current reigning king is the only person known to possess the release of this curse on these two people.'

'The skeleton in the old woman's cottage,' said Chris. 'That's the royal sorcerer.'

'Of course,' said Joel. 'But if it was hundreds of years ago then why not ask your father to release these people?' he asked. 'If the story is true then these people have surely paid their due. They were only doing good after all.'

'And release magic back into the kingdom? No,' said Dorian. 'No king will risk that ever again. Knowing there are potions out there that can cause harm is bad enough. The idea of allowing full-blown wizardry is just not worth thinking about.'

Joel looked the figures over and he was aware of the jewellery they both wore, thinking it looked out of place for this world, and in a strange way, familiar.

Caitlin began to yawn, quickly followed by Chris.

'I'm feeling sleepy,' she said.

'Me too,' said Joel.

'This is weird. I've never felt sleepy in my dreams before,' said Chris.

'Me neither,' Joel added.

'I think it's your own way of saying it's time to go home. You've done what you came here to do. You defeated your own self-doubts, you fought off your enemies, you rescued Freya, and I managed to find my way back, thanks to your smoothie,' said Dorian. 'It's time you went back too.'

The three siblings sat themselves down next to the pond and leaned against its wall, fatigue taking over rapidly.

'But will we ever see you again,' Caitlin asked Dorian, her eyes already shut.

'I hope so,' he replied. 'This is your dream after all. Your dreams are what you make them, right?'

'Right.'

Joel took hold of his necklace to give it back as he struggled to keep his eyes from closing.

'No,' said Dorian. 'It is yours now. It makes us family. Keep them. That way you'll find it easier to visit when you want to.'

'Cool,' mumbled Chris as he tried in vain to stifle a yawn.

'Thank you,' whispered Joel as his head drooped to one side.

Dorian knelt in front of them all.

'No. Thank you. You saved Freya, and in turn, have saved me. Sleep well, my friends. Until the next time.'

Joel, Chris, and Caitlin leant against one another; their eyes closed as tight as they had ever been.

Seconds later, they were fast asleep.

When they woke up the first thing they heard was the front door letterbox slamming closed. All three slowly sat up in their beds and they looked at one another, smiling, happy that they had returned safely.

Chris jumped out of his bed and ran to the window. He watched as the postman got back into his van and drove off.

'It was just the postman,' he said.

'What an adventure!' Caitlin cried. 'Can we do it again?'

'Cor, you're keen,' said Chris.

'It was the best. I've had a great time.' She ran to Joel and hugged him tightly.

'You're the best brothers, ever. And you didn't leave me behind.'

'No. I didn't, did I?' replied Joel, feeling pleased with himself.

'Well, I'm famished,' said Chris. 'who's for pancakes and ice cream?'

'Me!' shouted Caitlin as she ran out of the bedroom chasing Chris to the kitchen.

'And me,' yelled Joel hoping they heard him.

Joel lay back down on his bed and recounted the amazing journey he, his brother and sister had just had. He laughed as he remembered the creatures of the forest and the way Pratt and the Black Knight got trodden on by Pinky.

He hoped for more incredible adventures like this one, but for now he was glad to be home.

He reached for the photograph on his bedside cabinet. He smiled as he looked at his happy parents, wondering if indeed they were Dream Weavers just like he, Chris, and Caitlin.

And then he frowned.

He looked carefully at his mother and the necklace she was wearing.

He couldn't believe it. The female statue in the pond. She had the same necklace.

The large ring on his dad's middle finger in the picture – the male statue wore the same one.

'No way!' he muttered. 'They aren't wizards. It's mum and dad.'

Joel sat bolt upright and shouted as loud as he could.

'Chris! Caitlin! Forget the pancakes. It's time for bed! We're going on a rescue mission.'

Maynard Tait

Printed in Great Britain
by Amazon